TALES
GROSS
AND
GRUESOME

By Ellen Steiber

BULLSEYE BOOKS
Random House   New York

Copyright © 1995 by Ellen Steiber
Cover art copyright © 1995 by Broeck Steadman

Library of Congress Cataloging-in-Publication Data
Steiber, Ellen, 1955–
Tales of the gross and gruesome / by Ellen Steiber.
p. cm.
CONTENTS: Abracadaver—Killer bees—The ghastly coachman—The itch—Planet
Gross—The woman in white—The witch cat—Shelter.
ISBN 0-679-86846-1 (pbk.)
1. Ghost stories, American.   2. Children's stories, American.
[1. Ghosts—Fiction.   2. Short stories.]   I. Title.
PZ7.S81766St   1995
[Fic]—dc20
94-3764

RL: 5.4
First Bullseye Books edition: April 1995

Manufactured in the United States of America   10 9 8 7 6 5 4 3 2 1

CONTENTS

For Robin Sickafoose,
who showed me my first video game

Author's Note

Many people helped me with the stories in this book.
Thanks to: Joan Slattery and Cylin Busby for inspired
editing; Thomas Harlan Jr. for assuring me that I could
change video game software; Doug Lantz for all the
climbing info (and for actually climbing Abracadaver);
Robin Roche and Sanford Eigenbrode at the University
of Arizona's Department of Entomology for bee and
tarantula facts; "Big" Jim Griffith for Southwestern
folktales; and Wendy Froud, Gwen Stone, Ros Levinson,
and Jacqueline Floyd-Walker of Chagford, England, for
the ghost stories of Dartmoor.

THE ITCH

It was a hot, muggy August night when the air conditioning in Michael Turner's house broke down. Michael immediately announced to his parents that he couldn't take the heat in his upstairs bedroom. He'd sleep outside in the backyard instead.

"Fine," his mother replied. "You can set up the tent, just in case it rains."

"It won't rain," Michael assured her. His mother worried too much.

Michael dragged his sleeping bag out into the yard, plunked it down on the cool grass, and fell asleep instantly. He woke up in the morning, feeling great. He'd been right. It hadn't rained.

But Michael didn't feel great for long. As he set off for his summer job, coaching little kids in tennis, his face began to itch like crazy. He ran his finger along the side of his nose. There was definitely a bump there. *A mosquito must have got me,* he thought as he scratched and scratched.

Michael started off the morning by trying to

explain scoring to the five-year-olds. The kids were restless. Maybe that's because Michael was restless himself. He kept scratching the side of his nose. He couldn't help it. The itch was getting worse and worse. It got so bad that he went into the parks office and put on some calamine lotion. He looked silly with a pink nose, but it helped—for about ten minutes. Then the itching started up again, even stronger than before.

By the time Michael got home that day, the side of his face was bright red from all his scratching.

"Michael!" his mother said. "What have you done to your poor face?"

"It's no big deal, Mom," Michael replied. "A mosquito got me last night."

"Well, don't scratch it anymore," his mother told him. "It could get infected."

Michael had heard that skin will sometimes stop itching if you treat it either with ice or with very hot water. So first, he took the hottest shower he could stand. Then he put an ice pack on his face. But neither worked.

That night, the itching became even more intense. By the time Michael went to sleep, it wasn't only the bump on the side of his nose that itched, but the entire area around his eyes and nose. All night long he tossed and turned, trying not to scratch. He counted sheep, rubbed his face against his pillow, and reread his favorite comic books.

Morning came at last, and Michael leapt out of bed, relieved that he didn't have to lie there anymore, scratching and thinking about scratching. He had a tennis tournament today, one he'd been practicing a long time for. That would take his mind off this crazy itch.

He put on his white shorts and his lucky T-shirt and went downstairs. His eyes and cheeks were swollen, and the skin on his face was bright red.

"Good heavens!" his mother said. "It looks like you've had a brush with some poison ivy. Maybe we should get you to a doctor for an antihistamine."

"No way," Michael said, swigging a glass of orange juice. "Got a tournament today. Don't worry, I'll be fine."

Michael was the first one on the court that day. *All I need is a good match,* he told himself. *I just need to concentrate on something besides this stupid itch.*

Michael played his hardest. He also played his worst. He just couldn't concentrate on the match. All he could think about was the itch on his face, which was driving him wild.

He left the court before the tournament was over. He went straight home. Luckily, his mother was there. He found her sitting at her desk, paying bills.

"Mom," Michael said, "I think maybe I should see the doctor."

His mother looked up from the desk and bit back a shriek. "Oh, Michael," she said, "I can barely see your eyes—they're almost swollen shut. And those scratches…you look like you got in a fight with a mountain lion."

"Thanks a lot, Mom," Michael said. "Could we go to the doctor now?"

His mother nodded, grabbed her purse, and drove Michael straight to the doctor's office.

Michael fidgeted nervously in the waiting room. *Just a little while longer,* he told himself. *Dr. Harding will examine me and give me something to stop the itching. In an hour this will all be over.*

But things didn't go quite as Michael thought they would. Dr. Harding examined

Michael's face, then peered into his eyes, ears, nose, and mouth.

"Hmmm," he said.

"What?" Michael asked impatiently. "Is it poison ivy?"

"This isn't poison ivy," the doctor said. "Or an insect bite."

"How about an allergy?" Mrs. Turner suggested.

Dr. Harding frowned at Michael and shook his head. "Nope, doesn't look like allergies, either. I don't know what your problem is."

"This isn't very helpful," Michael mumbled as he scratched at his face.

"Can't you give him *something?*" Mrs. Turner asked the doctor.

"Well, I'll try an antihistamine," Dr. Harding said. "But I think Michael's problem may be psychological." He went on as if Michael weren't even in the room. "You must understand that the teen years are difficult. A twelve-year-old boy might manifest all sorts of odd physical symptoms while he's dealing with change. I'm going to give you the name of another doctor."

"Wait a minute," Michael said suspiciously. "This other doctor—is he a shrink?"

"She is a psychiatrist," Dr. Harding answered as he began to write a name and address on a piece of paper. "And I'd advise you to see her at once. In the meantime"—he winked at Michael—"don't scratch."

Four hours later Michael was sitting in a deep leather chair across from Dr. Andrea Randall.

"Are you happy, Michael?" Dr. Randall asked.

"No, I'm not happy. I'm going out of my mind!" Michael replied as he scratched furiously at his face. His mother had gotten him the antihistamine Dr. Harding had prescribed. It hadn't done any good at all. The itch was getting worse by the second. He was about two steps away from tearing the flesh off his face.

"Let's talk about your relationship with your parents," Dr. Randall said patiently.

Michael didn't answer. He had more important things to deal with. He turned away from Dr. Randall and scratched at his face until his fingernails were bloody.

Though Michael had done his best to ignore the shrink, that night he began to wonder if maybe he should have paid attention. Because as far as he could tell, he was definitely losing his mind. All he could think about was the itch and scratching, or not scratching, it. Everything else in his world seemed to have disappeared. The itch was the only thing that mattered. It was the only thing there was.

Michael woke the next morning with his pillow bloody and his face covered with deep gashes. In the bathroom, he cleaned up as best he could, but he knew it was useless. His face was beginning to look like something out of a horror movie.

He tried to sneak out that morning without his mother seeing him. But she called out to him as he was halfway across the lawn.

"Stop right there, young man!" she ordered. "You'll terrorize those poor five-year-olds if you show up at the park looking like that."

Michael had to agree. He went back into the house, called the parks office, and explained that he wouldn't be coming in to work. Then he went up to his room so he could at least sit through his agony in private.

One hour later Michael heard a knock on the

door of his room. He opened it to see his mother and Dr. Randall standing there, both looking concerned.

"What's she doing here?" he asked his mother.

"I came to see how you're doing," the psychiatrist answered.

"I'm afraid he'll scratch his eyes out," Michael's mother said in a worried tone.

Michael slammed the door in their faces. A stressed-out mother and a dopey psychiatrist were the last things he needed right now.

Outside his room, he heard his mother and Dr. Randall speaking in low voices. Then he heard them going back downstairs. Twenty minutes later the door to his room opened, and two men in white jackets walked in.

"We're here to take you to the hospital," the taller man said in an eerie, flat tone.

"What?" Michael yelped.

"Dr. Randall and your mother are afraid you might damage yourself if you stay here," the man explained. "We're going to take you in for observation."

Michael tried to argue, but the two men weren't listening. Before he knew it, they'd carried him out of the house and into a waiting ambulance.

"Stop!" Michael shrieked as the ambulance set off for the hospital. "You can't do this to me!"

"You're getting hysterical, son," the second orderly said. "Now just calm down or we'll be forced to put restraints on you."

Michael couldn't believe this was happening to him. It was straight out of a nightmare. "Let me out of this ambulance!" he screamed. Desperate, he began to fight, kicking and punching as hard as he could.

He arrived at the hospital in a straitjacket, which was the worst torment of all. Now there was no way he could scratch the itch. He was bundled into a hospital bed. Doctors, nurses, and orderlies peered at Michael, wrote notes on clipboards, and walked away briskly.

Michael yelled for the nurse. "Let me out of the straitjacket," he pleaded when a stern-looking woman appeared in his doorway. "Just for a few minutes. Please!"

"We'll take you out when it's time for your bath," she informed him.

Never in his life had Michael wanted a bath

as much as he wanted this bath. He counted the minutes. He imagined soaking in a tub of steaming hot water. Most of all, he pictured sinking his fingernails into the skin on his face.

Hours later, two nurses returned with a small basin of water and a sponge. "Time for your bath," said the stern-looking one. She held up the basin. "There's a baking soda solution in here that should make you feel better." She nodded at the younger nurse, who began to undo the straps on the straitjacket.

"Thank you," Michael said in what he hoped was a calm voice. Then, before either of the nurses could stop him, he ripped into his face with both hands. This time, he tore away thick chunks of flesh.

He actually felt a few seconds of relief—and then the young nurse began to scream and scream. And the stern one was backing away from him with a look of horror on her face. "Oh my God, I've heard about this," she said.

"What?" Michael asked. He'd never seen anyone look as repulsed as the nurse did.

"They crawl up into your nose and lay their eggs inside you," she said, her voice shaking.

"What?" Michael screamed. "What does? Tell me!"

The younger nurse began to gag. "I'm—I'm going to be sick!" she gasped, and ran for the bathroom.

Desperate, Michael grabbed the mirror from his bedside stand. In horror, he stared at his swollen, torn face. The skin was gone. Lodged in the red pulpy flesh beneath his cheekbone was a mass of tiny white eggs. And out of them were crawling hundreds of tiny black spiders!

SHELTER

"I don't believe it!" Holly Rudner said as she watched the Trent's Teen Tours bus pull away from the village square. "They left without us!"

Beside her, Alec Williams, a lanky boy with blue eyes and thick black hair, gave a lazy shrug. Alec was one of the few British kids on the tour of England; most of the teens were Americans. "Trent's such a mess, he won't even notice we're gone until tomorrow," Alec said.

"You're probably right," Holly agreed. Trent, their tour leader, was the most unorganized person she'd ever met. Her parents had been totally sold by his slick brochure and his charming English accent. But Holly had had a bad feeling about this trip from the start. By the third day of the tour, Trent had managed to lose their bus twice. And now she and Alec were lost.

"Look," Alec said, "we know that Bath is the next stop on the tour. We'll just take public transport and catch up with them there." He glanced at the bus schedule that was posted in the village square. "The only problem," he went on, "is that today is Sunday and the buses here don't run on Sunday. We can't get a bus out until tomorrow. I reckon we can stay at a bed-and-breakfast tonight."

But the bed-and-breakfasts in the tiny Devon village were all booked up. "Great," Holly said after they'd been turned away from the last one. She was stranded in a foreign country with a boy she barely knew. "Now what?"

"It's really not a tragedy," Alec told her. "I mean, don't you think this is a lot more interesting than that stupid tour?"

"If we'd stayed with that 'stupid tour,' we'd at least have a place to sleep tonight," Holly pointed out. "The weather report said it's supposed to rain. It's already drizzling."

"That doesn't mean anything. It's always drizzling in England," Alec assured her. "Listen," he continued, "when our bus came into town, I saw an old ruined farmhouse about a mile and a half back. It definitely looked deserted. We can spend the night there, hike back into the village in the morning, and be in Bath by afternoon."

Holly sighed. She really didn't have a better idea.

So she and Alec bought some biscuits and soda in the one store that was open on Sunday and then began following the narrow road that wound out of the village.

As they walked farther from the center of the village, the houses were spaced farther and farther apart. The road narrowed into a lane edged by two stone walls that were covered with ivy and wild berries.

Holly kept peering over the walls, looking for the farmhouse Alec had described. To the left of the lane was woodland—dark, lush green oaks and rowans with a thick growth of fern covering the ground. The land to the right was farmland—soft, hilly fields dotted with grazing sheep and cows. Even in the gray weather, Holly found herself impressed by the beauty of the countryside.

It was only when they were a good ways out of the village that Holly noticed that she felt uneasy. She shut her eyes, hating what was happening. She'd had feelings like this before. This was her secret, the thing she'd never admitted to anyone. She was, as she thought of it, "sort of psychic"—not enough to predict the future, but enough to know when something was seriously wrong. She stood still, trying to pinpoint the reason for her feeling.

We're not alone, she realized with a shiver. *There's someone—or something else out here.*

It was the noise, a crunching sound on the blacktop behind them, that felt so wrong. *Footsteps,* she thought, *and another sound—like the clinking of metal.* Holly turned around and saw only empty road.

"What is it?" Alec asked.

"I don't know," she said. "I thought I heard something behind us."

Alec turned around and looked. "Trees," he said dryly. "Very unusual in the English countryside."

"No, I heard something," Holly insisted. "Footsteps and some kind of metal rattling. Didn't you hear it?"

"Not me," Alec said with a grin. "I just heard the usual ghosts and vampires whispering back there."

Holly gave him a suspicious look. "Aren't we getting out near the moor?"

Their tour bus had crossed the moor earlier

that morning. It was wild land—wide open, rolling hills beneath a gray sky that seemed to go on forever. There wasn't anything out there except grass and stones and wild ponies. Holly didn't know why, but the moor spooked her. It was somehow bleak and frightening.

"The moor's a bit of a walk yet," Alec said cheerfully. He gave her a sideways look. "What's wrong?"

"It's—it's just kind of creepy out there," Holly confessed.

"That it is," Alec agreed. "There are supposed to be all sorts of *creeeeepy* things on the moor."

"Like what?" Holly asked.

"Like the hairy hands," he replied, holding his hands up like curved claws. "See, when you're driving across the moor, these hairy hands are supposed to suddenly appear and wrench the steering wheel from you," he explained. "Then—*crash!*"

"That's ridiculous," Holly said. "Besides, it wasn't *hands* following us. I heard footsteps."

"Maybe it's the hairy feet, then," Alec teased. "Or the witch who's supposed to lure travelers to their deaths in the bogs."

"Just find the barn," Holly said crossly. "How far did you say it was?"

"About a mile and a half."

It occurred to Holly that Alec was a lousy judge of distance. They'd been walking for over an hour. They had to have gone at least three miles by now. The road had twisted and turned more times than she could count. And there were almost no houses now. Just fields and trees on either side.

The afternoon was growing chilly. Holly knew it would be dark soon. She definitely didn't want to be out near the moor in the dark. And she still heard it: the sound of footsteps and the metallic clinking behind them.

"Aha!" Alec suddenly cried. "We're here. And it's better than a barn," he said in the exaggerated tones of a game-show host. "It's a Devon longhouse!"

Holly knew from Trent's rambling lecture that Devon longhouses combined house and barn in one building. Most were massive stone structures at least 300 years old.

She swung herself up onto the wall and gazed at the place where they'd be spending the night. This Devon longhouse was in terrible shape. All of the walls were crumbling. Depending on where you looked, the thatched roof was either caved in or missing entirely. The windows and the door were long gone.

"Oh, this should be terrific shelter," Holly said. "We'll be lucky if it doesn't collapse on us."

"Do you have a better idea?" Alec asked.

Holly shook her head. The sun was almost completely gone now, and she was chilled. She knew that being inside the ruined farmhouse would be better than nothing.

Alec, who was still on the other side of the wall, said, "Why don't you make yourself at home? I'm going to pick some of these black-berries for dessert."

Holly approached the ruined farmhouse cautiously. The closer she got, the worse it looked. A huge, ancient oak tree stood in front of the house, skeletal in the dying light. Holly shook herself as she walked past it; even the tree gave her the creeps.

A stone set into the base of the building bore the number 1590. The building was over 400 years old, she realized. A funny smell came through the open door. Holly stopped as another thought occurred to her: *Lots of people and animals must have died here over the last four centuries. This place has definitely seen death.*

From the open doorway, she surveyed their "home" for the night. To her left was the part of the building that must have been the barn. She could see the remains of stalls and a hayloft. A stone trough was set into the floor. A wide passageway separated the barn from the house section.

Gingerly, Holly stepped inside a large rectangular room that must have once been the kitchen. A deep stone sink took up one wall, a huge hearth another. It had clearly been ages since anyone had lived here. The house was cold and damp and smelled of mildew and rot. And it was making Holly very nervous.

We shouldn't stay here, she thought. *This place isn't good. We shouldn't be here at all.*

Maybe, she thought, *I could persuade Alec to camp out under a tree for the night.* An ominous crack of thunder quickly ruled out that possibility.

She whirled as she heard the now-familiar sounds behind her—the footsteps and the metallic clink. But this time she smiled, as she

19

finally saw what was causing them. A large black dog—mostly Labrador retriever, she guessed—stood just a few feet from her. Its tail was wagging. A blackened metal tag hung from its chain collar; that must be what caused the clinking sound, she realized.

"So it was you who followed us," she said, feeling relieved. The dog came up and stood beside her, clearly wanting to be petted. Holly ran her hand across its sleek head. "Good thing you showed up. We could use some company tonight." She reached for the metal tag—there were letters on it, but they were so worn all she could make out was a J and an O.

Tail still wagging, the dog curled up against the far wall of the barn. Holly pulled a sweater out of her pack, feeling a little better. She was glad the dog was there. What was it the old folktales said about dogs and cats? Something about their being able to see ghosts. If there was something weird here, the dog would let her know.

Alec stepped through the doorway, his baseball cap filled with blackberries. "Dessert has arrived!" he announced. He stopped and looked around the dilapidated longhouse. "Just like a five-star hotel," he murmured. "It's got atmosphere, antiquity—"

"And ants," Holly finished. "Not to mention mosquitoes, flies, roaches—and a very large dog."

"Where?" Alec asked.

Holly turned to introduce him to the dog, but the dog was gone. "He was here a moment ago," she said. "Real friendly. Looked like a black Lab, except bigger."

Alec's blue eyes widened. "Ooooh," he said in a spooky voice. "One of the wraith dogs of the moor."

"You're crazy," Holly said. "He was a sweetie. But I guess he didn't want to sleep here, either. This place is gross."

Alec glanced around. "The barn is the safest bet," he said. "Less chance of the roof caving in on us."

"We ought to try to clean some of this muck off the floor before it gets too dark to see what we're doing," Holly said.

Alec nodded, grabbed a stick from the debris on the floor, and began scraping at one of the corners. "This is going to take hours," he said after a few minutes. "I've got a better solution."

"What's that?" Holly asked.

"Bracken," Alec said. "Ferns. They grow wild all over the moor. I've got me trusty Swiss Army knife; all I have to do is go cut some bracken, and it'll be better than sleeping on goose down."

"Right," Holly said. By this point she'd learned not to take everything Alec said too seriously. Still, even if bracken didn't feel anything like down, sleeping on it would be better than sleeping on the moldy floor.

"Want to come along?" Alec asked.

"No thanks."

"Back in ten," Alec promised. He left the longhouse as another crack of thunder boomed through the sky. This one was definitely closer.

Hurry up, Alec, Holly thought. It was almost dark now, and she didn't like the idea of him being out there alone in a storm. And she didn't much like being left alone in the house. Well, not quite alone. The dog had to be here somewhere.

I should have gone with Alec, Holly thought. Because the feeling was back, stronger than ever—that creepy feeling that they shouldn't be here at all.

You're being totally irrational, Holly scolded

herself. But she couldn't help it. She was sure that there was something else in the house—something besides herself and Alec and a large black dog.

Holly stiffened as she heard a noise. It wasn't footsteps this time, but the sound of a door swinging on its hinges. That was definitely strange. As far as she could tell, all the doors in the house had fallen off long ago.

Maybe it's one of the trees creaking in the wind, she told herself. She jumped as the "door" slammed shut.

Calm down, Holly told herself. *Get your flashlight and find out what's making that noise.*

She whirled as she heard the sound of the dog's nails clicking against a stone floor. The dog wasn't anywhere in sight, and if there'd ever been a stone floor in the house, it was buried under at least a foot of muck.

"I'm imagining things," Holly said aloud. "I'm cold and tired and scared, and I'm letting my imagination run away with me."

She shut her eyes as she felt a cold nose press against her palm. Was she imagining that too? No—she opened her eyes and there was the dog, black tail wagging.

"Bracken delivery for Ms. Rudner!" Alec called out. Seconds later he entered the longhouse, almost completely hidden behind the thick bundle of ferns in his arms.

"You're just in time to meet the dog," Holly said, hoping her voice didn't betray just how freaked she'd been.

Alec peered through the ferns. "Where is he?"

"Right here," Holly said. But the dog was gone again. "I swear he was here," she insisted.

"Uh-huh," Alec said. "Was Santa Claus here, too?"

Alec began to lay the ferns on the floor of the barn. As he did, Holly heard the sound of the dog's tag clinking against his chain collar.

"Alec—do you hear that sound?" she asked.

Alec listened. "I hear rain," he replied.

"I'll show you the dog," Holly said, getting tired of Alec's not believing her. She turned toward the kitchen.

It was dark in the house now. She switched on her flashlight as she heard the dog's collar clinking. He was lying near the hearth.

"There you are," Holly said, walking toward him. "I want you to come meet Alec."

She froze as she heard a door swinging open again. The dog's ears lifted at the sound and a low growl came from his throat.

"At least you hear it, too," Holly said.

Somewhere in the house without doors, a door slammed shut. The dog stood up, ears cocked.

"Alec!" Holly called. "Would you come here for a moment?"

A few seconds later, Alec walked into the kitchen. "What's up?" he asked.

Holly pointed to the fireplace. "There," she said. "The dog."

Alec shone his flashlight at the hearth. "Where?"

"You don't see him?"

"You do?"

Holly was really starting to get scared now. The dog was standing right there. How could Alec not see it? Was he putting her on? Or was she hallucinating?

"Come here, boy," Holly said to the dog. "Come here."

The door slammed again, and now Holly heard footsteps—heavy footsteps. She looked around. She didn't see anyone, but the footsteps were getting closer. A low rumble started in the dog's chest.

"Alec," Holly said. "You don't see the dog? And you haven't heard the footsteps or the door slamming shut?"

"There aren't any doors here," Alec said patiently. "Or dogs. It's just you and me here, got it?"

Holly didn't get it. None of this was making sense. The only thing that was clear was that the feeling of danger was even stronger now, like a flashing red warning light.

"Alec." Holly's voice was shrill with fear. "We've got to get out of here now. This place is dangerous."

"Are you daft?" Alec retorted. "It's raining, into this kitchen as a matter of fact, and I just set up a dry place for us to sleep."

"Please!" she said.

"No," he replied, and went back toward the barn.

The footsteps were coming closer. Holly stood paralyzed with fear, getting colder and wetter as rain fell through the broken roof. She couldn't take her eyes off the dog. He knew there was something in the house. His head swerved toward the sound of the footsteps and his hackles rose. The dog was their only protection.

"Come on," she said in a shaky voice. "Let's go into the barn with Alec."

To her surprise, the dog did as she asked, trotting to her side and following her from the kitchen into the barn.

Alec sat on the bed of ferns, studying a map by flashlight. He looked up as Holly approached.

"Tired of getting soaked in the kitchen?" he asked.

Holly put her hand on the dog's warm, silky head. "You still don't see the dog?" she asked.

"Yes, I see the dog," Alec said in an exasperated tone. "He's standing right next to the Easter bunny!"

In the other part of the house, a door opened and slammed shut, and Holly whirled. The footsteps grew louder. Someone was walking slowly, deliberately, from the kitchen into the barn. The dog began to growl again. And then she heard something else, a booming one-word command. "Now!"

Instantly, the dog sprang forward, knocking Alec to the floor.

"What the—?" Alec's words turned into a terrified scream. Holly ran toward them, but she wasn't fast enough. A stream of bright red blood washed over her as the dog's jaws closed on Alec's throat.

"Stop!" Holly screamed. She reached for the dog's collar, determined to pull him off. Her hands closed on air. The dog was gone as if it had never been. But at her feet lay Alec, unconscious and bleeding.

Holly made her way toward the village, tears running down her cheeks. She'd used her sweater to bandage Alec as best she could. Now she had to get him help. If she didn't, he'd die. She was sure of that.

Why had they chosen to spend the night in a place so far from town? she asked herself. And why hadn't she listened to her instincts—why had she ever gone into the longhouse at all? And what, she wondered, would she tell the police when she did get help—that Alec had been attacked by an invisible dog?

She pressed herself against the wall on the side of the lane as bright headlights shone behind her. She was surprised when the car slowed. A cheerful-looking woman rolled down her window.

"Need a lift?" she inquired. "It's a nasty night to be out walking in the lanes. My name is Claire."

Holly waited just an instant to be sure, but she didn't sense anything dangerous in this woman. She climbed into the car. "I need to get into town," she said, wondering how much she should say.

"That's where I'm going, too," Claire said. "Where were you, then?"

"My friend and I were stranded," Holly began. "So we decided to spend the night in an abandoned longhouse, just a little ways back. And—"

Claire cut her off, her voice filled with disbelief. "You spent the night at the old Wheeler place?" She slowed the car and her eyes searched Holly's. "You said you had a friend," she said. "What happened to her?"

"Him," Holly said. "He's still there—and I've got to get him help."

"I'll say." Claire began driving as fast as the twisting lane allowed. "You chose the wrong spot for a hotel," she told Holly. "The village has been trying to get permission to raze that building for years. It's haunted, you know. Fred Wheeler was the last man who lived there. He died in 1857. But before he did, he went a little crazy. He used to have a big black hunting dog by the name of Jacko."

Jacko, Holly thought, remembering the dog's worn metal tag, with the J and the O.

"One night, during a heavy rain," Claire went on, "a young man who was passing through spent the night in Wheeler's barn without asking. Wheeler found him there and loosed Jacko on him."

"What do you mean?" Holly asked.

"I mean he ordered the dog to tear the man's throat out." Claire stopped the car as they came to the village police station. "Let's get your friend some help, and then I'll tell you the rest of the story."

Four hours later, Holly sat in a hallway at the local hospital. Claire was still by her side, waiting with her until Alec got out of the operating room.

Finally, a doctor approached them. "Your friend Alec's lost a lot of blood and will have to

30

stay here for a few days," he said. "But we expect he'll be fine."

Holly felt herself go weak with relief.

"Come on," Claire said gently. "You can sleep on my couch tonight, and then I'll get you to Bath tomorrow, so you don't have to stop in any more haunted houses."

As they left the hospital, Holly remembered that she still hadn't heard the rest of the story. "So what happened?" she asked. "With Mr. Wheeler?"

"They hung him and the dog," Claire said. "They hung them both from that big old oak tree right in front of the house. But everyone who lives around here knows they never should have hanged them on that land."

"What do you mean?" Holly asked.

"Well, that they're both still there, on that land, in that house. At least their ghosts are. And they're just waiting for the next person who's fool enough to take shelter there."

THE GHASTLY COACHMAN

"Why can't we just go straight to the beach?" Addie Tanner asked as her mother drove between two stone gateposts onto a long tree-covered drive.

"The beach can wait for a day," her mother answered. "You've never met your great-aunt, and we're only staying overnight. We'll still have nearly two weeks at the beach."

"Yeah, yeah," Addie said. She knew she was being rude, but she couldn't help it. The two weeks her family spent at the beach every summer were the best part of the year. She didn't want to give up a day of vacation to visit some old lady she just happened to be related to.

"Addie, don't be a baby about this," her father chided. "Your Great-Aunt Emmeline's house is one of the finest examples of pre–Civil War architecture in the entire South. You're very lucky to get a chance to stay here."

Addie had already heard all of that about forty times. She was about to say so when the house came into view. Addie caught her breath as she stared at the great white three-story home, with its tall, slender marble columns and wide stairway. It was like something out of a movie—or a dream. She wouldn't have been surprised if the door had opened and women in floor-length dresses had swept out on their way to a ball.

Instead the door opened and a small, white-haired woman in a pink jogging suit smiled at them. "Well, you've finally made it," she called out.

Addie grabbed her daypack and got out of the car. The air here smelled like honeysuckle. She walked up the long flight of stairs and waited awkwardly as Great-Aunt Emmeline greeted her parents.

Finally, Emmeline turned to her, her blue eyes bright with curiosity. "My, my," the old woman said softly. "So this is the girl who was named for my own dear sister, Adeleine. I can't believe this is the first time we've actually met." Emmeline looked into Addie's eyes, and Addie realized that she and her great-aunt were exactly the same height. Addie was on the small side for a twelve-year-old. She wondered if the first Adeleine had been as short.

Emmeline put an arm around Addie. "Come inside, and I'll show you the house," she offered.

Emmeline's "house" was a mansion, and it was magnificent. The floors were marble, the ceiling moldings trimmed in gold. The chairs and couches were covered in silk, and thick velvet curtains draped the tall windows. Every room had crystal vases filled with flowers—lilacs, jasmine, orchids, and pure white calla lilies.

Addie followed her aunt through a dining room, a drawing room, two parlors, a ballroom, a sewing room, a music room, a morning room, and a library.

And then Emmeline began a tour of the grounds. There were gardens, a greenhouse that Emmeline called the conservatory, a barn, a stable with two handsome geldings, a pond, and a carriage house with three beautiful old carriages.

"This is the carriage that took my great-grandparents to their wedding," Emmeline said, pointing to a beautiful white carriage with green trim.

"And this," she said, indicating a smaller carriage with polished wood sides, "is the one my great-grandparents used for going to town."

The third carriage, a small one with red pin-stripe paint, was "the ladies' coach," Emmeline explained. "The ladies used to travel in it to visit their neighbors."

"Sounds like there was a coach for every purpose," Addie's father said.

"Just about," Emmeline agreed.

That night, Addie stayed in the bedroom Emmeline and her sister Adeleine had shared as teenagers. It was an airy room on the third floor with two four-poster beds and a window seat that looked out over the back of the house.

Addie changed into an oversized T-shirt, then curled up on the window seat. She parted the lace curtains and opened the window. A cool evening breeze blew in, carrying the scent of honeysuckle. Beneath a full moon, the gazebo shone white. Except for the sound of crickets, the night was perfectly silent. A few minutes later, Addie sank down into the bed that was closer to the window and fell asleep.

She never knew what woke her. But something made her open her eyes and sit up in bed. The room was dark. It was still the middle of the night. And the scent of honeysuckle was stronger than ever. Addie shrugged and was about to burrow down beneath the covers again when she heard it.

It was a strange crunching sound coming from outside. Curious, Addie got up. Kneeling on the window seat, she peered out the open window. The full moon was high overhead now, bathing the estate in bright silver light. Addie could easily make out the rows of vegetables in the gardens, the white latticework of the gazebo, and the gravel path that circled the house. There was something else directly outside her window, something that hadn't been there that day—a gleaming black carriage drawn by four tall black horses. Addie didn't know why, but the sight of it sent a wave of fear straight through her. She shivered, wondering why the sight of an old coach should fill her with such dread.

Because it shouldn't be there, she realized. Something about the coach was wrong. She didn't remember having seen it in the carriage house that day. And why was it directly below her window?

She felt the fear get sharper. It was cutting through her now, as easily as the cool night air cut through her T-shirt.

Addie forced herself to look at the coach more closely. Shiny black wheels rested on the gravel path. *That must be what made the crunching sound,* she thought. Her eyes went to the front of the carriage. Two polished brass lamps shone. A man dressed in a black suit and a black top hat sat holding the reins.

What, she wondered, was an old-fashioned coach doing out there in the middle of the night? She knew the answer as soon as she'd asked the question: It was waiting for someone.

Almost as if he could feel her stare, the driver slowly turned and lifted his face toward her window. Addie drew back with a gasp. A jagged scar twisted the man's mouth to the side. But that wasn't what freaked her. The coachman's face was grotesque. He had only one good eye. In the other eye socket, a blank milky-white eyeball gleamed up at her. Addie stared at his deformed face, transfixed. The coachman terrified her, but she couldn't look away.

I wonder if he can see me, Addie thought with a shudder.

And then she knew that he could. Because he pointed a finger straight at her. "There's room for one more," he called out. "Room for one more!"

Without thinking, Addie slammed the window shut. She didn't know what the coachman meant and she didn't care. What she wanted was to run straight into her parents' room. But she couldn't. Her father would only tell her she was being a baby again. And this time she'd have to agree with him. She could go to Great-Aunt Emmeline, but somehow she didn't feel right about waking a seventy-year-old woman in the middle of the night.

Addie considered turning on the lights in her room—but then the coachman would be able to see right through the lace curtains.

She went over to the bed that was farther from the window. She couldn't get the image of the ghastly coachman out of her mind. She kept waiting to hear the sound of the wheels on the stone path as the carriage drove away. But the night was silent. Addie sat there in the pitch dark, her knees drawn close to her chest, shaking. She stayed that way until the first light of dawn filtered into the room. Then she finally let herself lie down and sleep again.

Addie pushed at the fruit on her plate. Normally, she was starving when she woke up.

But this morning she just wasn't hungry. Even Emmeline's corn fritters didn't tempt her. She looked around the sunny morning room, wondering if what she'd seen last night had been real.

"What's the matter, Addie?" her mother asked from across the table. "Aren't you feeling well?"

"I'm fine," Addie said. If her mother thought she was sick, she might put off going to the beach today. And there was no way Addie was going to stick around for a return visit from the black coach.

"Did you sleep well?" Emmeline asked.

"No," Addie said, unable to hold it in. "I saw something outside my window last night. It was this big black coach, pulled by four black horses. And the driver had this incredibly gross face. He was just sitting there on the gravel path beneath my window—"

"You must have been dreaming, dear," Emmeline interrupted. "There's no gravel path beneath that window. The back of the house is all grass."

Mr. Tanner chuckled and said, "Oh, Addie, you've always had a very active imagination."

"I think she's been watching too many of those awful horror movies," her mother said.

"I'm not making this up!" Addie said indignantly.

Great-Aunt Emmeline regarded her with serious blue eyes. "No, I don't believe you are," she said.

"A black coach," she went on thoughtfully. "That's very odd. I've never seen a black coach around here. I'll have to look into it."

"It's just a dream, honey," her mother said. "It will fade."

An hour later, all talk of Addie's nightmare was forgotten as she and her parents hugged Emmeline good-bye and set off for their summer vacation. Before they left, Addie took one last look from the bedroom window. Emmeline was right. There was no gravel path.

Addie spent the the first week and a half of vacation at the beach swimming, sunning, and windsurfing. Then the weather changed. A heavy mist settled over the beach town. It didn't actually rain, but it was gray and foggy.

Addie sat in the rented beach cottage, staring out the window. Her parents had gone off to a sailing museum. They'd invited her, but the truth was she'd rather watch TV reruns than go to a museum. She just couldn't believe that the weather had turned so lousy.

Addie called a couple of the kids she'd met on the beach, but no one was home. They were probably all at the sailing museum with their parents, she figured. So she finished the horror novel she was reading and wrote a postcard to Great-Aunt Emmeline. Then she watched some really dumb soap operas and an even dumber game show. Finally, when she was so bored she thought she'd scream, she decided to go to the boardwalk. She'd already been there a million times, but she could at least see if anyone interesting was hanging out.

For nearly an hour Addie wandered the boards. The fog was amazing. She could see the neon lights of the midway's rides, but not the white sand beach or the ocean beyond it. The waves breaking against the shore sounded muffled and far away. The scent of the salt air was strong, though. It mingled with the smells of the midway: cotton candy, popcorn, and fries.

Addie bought herself a soda and started down the midway. Even in the gloomy weather, crowds were lined up for the rides. Addie dug into her pocket. She had just enough money to go on one good ride. And she knew exactly which one she would choose.

Addie made her way toward the Death-Spin. It was one of the scariest rides on the midway. She watched from a distance as a new group walked through the blue entrance gate and onto the ride. Everyone took a place, standing against a circular wooden wall. They weren't strapped in. They just stood there. The ride started, and the circle began to spin faster and faster until it lifted itself up into the air. That's when the scary part started and the screams began—because the floor dropped out. The people on the Death-Spin would be spinning like mad, stuck to the wall with only centrifugal force to hold them in place. If the ride slowed at the wrong moment, they'd all fall.

Addie watched, fascinated, as the ride slowed, coming back down, and the screams stopped. Last year she hadn't been allowed to get on. There was a red line painted on a post beside the blue gate and a sign that said YOU HAVE TO BE THIS TALL TO GO ON THIS RIDE. Last year Addie had been one inch too short. She might

42

still be too short, but it was worth finding out. She walked up to the post and stood next to the red line.

"You're clear," said a good-looking boy who was standing near the gate.

"About time!" Addie said. She wished she could stand next to the boy on the ride, but there was a long line waiting behind him. They might not even get on in the same group.

Addie took a place at the end of the line. She waited anxiously as the blue gate swung open and the line inched forward. She couldn't believe she was doing this! She'd wanted to go on the Death-Spin for years. She kept her eyes on the boy as he took his place against the circular wall. She couldn't help feeling a little jealous as a pretty girl with long blond hair squeezed in beside him. There was still room on the other side of him, but the ride was nearly full.

Oh, please, Addie prayed, *let me get on this one!*

Her heart sank as she reached the front of the line just as the ticket taker swung the blue gate shut. "That's it!" he called out. "This one's full." He went toward the ride to start it up, but hesitated. Addie watched his thin back, hoping like mad that he could see that there was still a space next to the cute guy.

"Wait a minute," the ticket taker called. "There's one more space left."

Suddenly a strange feeling swept through Addie. She realized that it was because the smells of the ocean and the midway were gone—and in their place was the sweet, heady scent of honeysuckle.

Her eyes widened with terror as the ticket taker swung to face her. She hadn't really noticed him before. But he was dressed in black—black jeans, a black jacket, and a black baseball cap. And his face was exactly as she knew it would be: a jagged scar twisted his mouth to the side, and one blank milky-white eyeball rolled toward her.

The ticket taker pointed his finger straight at her. "There's room for one more," he said. "Room for one more."

"No," Addie said. She wanted to scream, but the scream was stuck in her throat. She couldn't believe what she was seeing. She stumbled backward through the crowd, the laugh of the ticket taker in her ears.

Addie ran till she was clear at the other end of the midway. Her heart still racing, she leaned against a T-shirt stand. She'd just about convinced herself that the ghastly coachman at Emmeline's house was a dream. Was this a dream, too? Or were both incidents real?

She shuddered, trying to talk sense to herself. *No one in this day and age goes around with an eye like that,* she reasoned. *It's probably one of those fake eyeballs that they sell on the boardwalk.* And it was probably just a coincidence that he used the words from her "dream." But what about the scent of honeysuckle? She'd smelled the honeysuckle before she'd seen him. Addie knew she hadn't imagined that.

Summoning all her courage, she decided to go back to the gate and take a second look at the man. At least that way she'd know whether or not she was imagining it.

But she never made it to the gate. The screams of the people on the Death-Spin reached a terrified pitch as the ride jerked to a halt while it was still in midair. Addie watched in disbelief and horror as everyone on the ride plummeted straight to the ground.

45

*　　*　　*

Addie had only been back from vacation a few days when she received a letter from Emmeline.

"Dear Addie," it read. "I was so worried about you after I heard about that terrible accident in the amusement park. Thank goodness you weren't on that ride!

"I checked with the local historical society about two things you mentioned. There *was* a gravel path where you saw one. From the year the house was built until the Civil War, a gravel path circled the house. But grass grew over it after the war. Somehow, my dear, you saw the grounds as they were during the first half of the nineteenth century.

"As for that black coach, I described it to Mrs. Carter, who runs the historical society. Then I asked if anyone around these parts owned something like it.

"'I assure you no one would want to keep one of those things,' Mrs. Carter replied. 'The coach your niece described was a funeral hearse.'"

ABRACADAVER

Nathan stared into the dying campfire. Even though it was mid-July, the night was cool in the mountains. On the other side of the fire, his Uncle Chris was sorting out climbing gear. They were camped at the base of the towering granite spires known as the Domes, one of the best climbing areas in the West. About fifty feet to Nathan's right was the start of the route he'd been wanting to climb for years: Abracadaver.

Nathan pulled a climbing guide out of his pack and hunched closer to the fire. For the zillionth time, he read a description of the route. All of Abracadaver was considered difficult, but it was the first three pitches—or segments of the climb—that were the hardest. There were places where the cracks in the rock were too wide to get a decent hold; others where the granite was loose and could slide out from under you at any second. "Boy, this guide tells you everything except how the route got its name," Nathan commented.

47

Chris squinted across the fire at him. "Trust me, you don't want to know."

Nathan groaned. "What do you mean, I don't want to know? What is it?"

"It's a ghost story," Chris warned.

"Ooooh, I'm terrified," Nathan said with a smirk.

Chris shrugged. "Okay. It's like this. The first ascent on this route was about twenty years ago. One of the climbers, Rich Morgan, was kind of a legend around here. Couldn't do anything wrong. Until he climbed this particular route."

"And then?" Nathan asked.

"He and his partner are halfway up the route when Rich pulls down a loose block of rock," Chris explained. "Rich falls and is injured so badly he can't stand. His partner gives him first aid. And then, just after sundown, a thunderstorm comes up out of nowhere and soaks them both. Rich begins to shiver and talk nonsense— like his mind is gone or something deep inside him is broken."

Nathan shrugged. "Bad luck, I guess."

Chris raised one eyebrow and went on with his story. "Well, Rich's partner is starting to worry that Rich might not make it through the night if he doesn't get some serious medical attention. So he tells Rich he's going to get help and he'll be back as soon as he can. He rappels down the rock and then starts the hike out to the road. But, as the story goes, the whole time he was traveling down, he could hear Rich screaming, 'Don't leave me alone up here! Please don't leave me alone!'"

Nathan poked at the embers. "That's supposed to be scary?"

"I'm not done yet," his uncle replied. "The next morning his partner gets back with a search team. Rich is gone. They find his climbing gear right where it was the night before and blood all over the place. But they never found the body."

"Did he fall off the ledge?" Nathan asked. "Maybe he hit the ground and a bear got him."

"That's what the sheriff thought," Chris admitted. "But usually, when a bear takes a man, it leaves some sort of trace. The body doesn't just up and vanish."

Nathan was starting to feel a little spooked, but he didn't want to admit it. "So how'd the route get its name?" he asked in what he hoped was a casual tone.

Chris took a pot of boiling water off the

embers and poured himself a cup of tea. "For the first few years after Rich disappeared, climbers kept expecting to find his cadaver. I mean, everyone was pretty sure the body was still up there somewhere, so they kind of made a joke of it by naming the route Abracadaver. But the joke died pretty fast."

"What do you mean?" Nathan asked.

"There've been a lot of weird stories about climbers hearing Rich's voice in the wind and rain," Chris answered. "They say he's waiting for another climber to die...so his ghost will have company."

The next morning Chris and Nathan woke at dawn, ate a quick breakfast, and broke camp.

Nathan gazed up at the clear blue sky. "We shouldn't get any of those thunderstorms today, right?"

"It's pretty unlikely," Chris said. "Thunderstorm season hasn't really started yet. Besides, I plan to have us off the rock by the afternoon, before the storms usually hit." He swatted Nathan on the shoulder. "Don't worry," he said. "You're a pretty solid climber—for a thirteen-year-old. We'll do fine."

Chris led the first pitch of the route, which was an off-width crack—too big for wedging in a finger or a fist, but too small to get your whole body into. Nathan followed, doing his best to copy his uncle's moves. It was strenuous, difficult climbing, but he kept at it, refusing to give in to fear.

It was exactly noon when Nathan and Chris pulled themselves over the lip of Lunch Ledge.

"Perfect timing," Chris said as he took some water and energy bars from his pack. "We'll have some lunch before starting the second half of the climb."

Nathan sat on the wide ledge, gazing out at the view below. He could see the shallow canyon that they'd hiked up yesterday to reach the base of the rock. They'd had an intense day, carrying all their gear as they scrambled up huge slabs of granite edged with mesquite and manzanita trees. Now the granite glistened white in the sun, and Nathan thought it was about the best view he'd ever seen. He was a little tired, but he felt good. He knew he'd done well on the hardest part of the climb.

"We'd better move if we're going to top out by this afternoon," Chris announced. He consulted his map, then said, "This next pitch isn't supposed to be as hard as the ones we just did, but don't get sloppy. You're leading and there's some loose rock up there."

"No problem," Nathan said.

The pitch started easily enough. Nathan felt his body moving with a sure, easy rhythm. Then, about twenty feet above Lunch Ledge, the cracks in the rock became shallow and crumbly.

This is not cool, Nathan thought as he set a little wedge-shaped piece of metal, known as a stopper, into the rock. He clipped the stopper to his rope, put some weight on it, realized it wouldn't hold him if he fell, and put a second stopper in. This one wasn't going to hold either. He wondered if he should turn back, or at least tell Chris he was having a hard time. No, he decided. They'd done the hardest part—the rest would be easier.

Nathan kept climbing. Ten feet later, he realized he was in major trouble. The footholds were small and crumbly—it was like standing on crackers. And he'd just stepped left when he should have gone right.

"Nathan!" Chris hollered. "Are you okay up there?"

"Fine!" Nathan lied as he frantically tried to hold on and recover. He tried to put in another stopper; this one wouldn't even stay in the rock. He looked at the wall of crumbling granite in front of him. His life had come down to one very simple choice: Climb or fall.

Taking a deep breath, Nathan reached out for a handhold—and watched in horror as it broke cleanly off the rock.

He was falling before he even knew what was happening. He glanced down between his feet. Lunch Ledge was coming toward him—fast.

Chris watched, terrified, as his nephew hurtled through space, then hit the ledge with a sickening crunch. Immediately, Nathan began screaming in agony.

Chris had never moved so fast in his life. He was at his nephew's side within minutes. Nathan was lying still, his face ash-white with pain.

"How you doing, bud?" Chris asked gently.

"I've been better," Nathan replied.

Chris winced as he saw that Nathan's left shoulder was badly mangled. "I'd say you've dislocated your shoulder," he said, touching it lightly. "Maybe broken it, too. And"—Chris looked at the boy's right foot, which was twisted completely backward—"it looks like you've got a broken foot or ankle."

"How am I going to get down?" Nathan asked, his voice trembling. "It really hurts."

"I know it does," Chris replied. He made sure that Nathan still had sensation in his fingers and toes. Then he got him into as comfortable a position as he could and covered him with an extra shirt he'd packed.

"I'm going to have to get help to get you to the ground," Chris said. He set a container of water beside Nathan. "Make sure you keep drinking water," he warned. "If you dehydrate, it will only make you weaker. And don't be scared. I'll be back ASAP."

Nathan's eyes were shut against the pain. "Just hurry," he said. "Please."

"I promise," Chris told him.

Chris knew he couldn't get Nathan down the way he'd come up. Nathan would have to be lowered in a stretcher, accompanied by a rescue worker. Their combined weight meant that they'd need the support of a fixed anchor, something much stronger than the stoppers he and

Nathan had used before. Without the fixed anchors, they could both be killed.

Chris checked the climbing guide. Sure enough, there were two fixed pitons on the ledge, driven into the rock as a safety measure by previous climbers. The pitons were supposed to be hidden behind a bush of some sort, but the ledge was fifty feet long, and brush was scattered from one end to the other. The fixed anchors could be anywhere, Chris realized as he began searching.

Chris cut short the search as he heard Nathan moan. He didn't have time to be poking through bushes, looking for rusted pitons. For all he knew, they weren't even here anymore.

Working fast, Chris made the best anchor he could from his own equipment. It wouldn't be strong enough to carry Nathan down later, but it would support his own weight. It would get him off the rock.

Chris began the rappel down. Getting to the bottom of the route wouldn't take long. But he still had a two-hour hike out of the canyon before he reached his truck, with its CB radio. He was near the bottom of the rock when he made the mistake of looking up. Chris thought nothing could be more frightening than watching Nathan fall, but now a new wave of fear shot straight into his gut.

Thunderclouds were building on the horizon.

Nathan bit down on his lip as another surge of pain went through him. The pain was like fire, burning all the time and then suddenly more searing than ever, as if someone had just fanned the flames. It was shooting through his left shoulder and down his arm. It was radiating from his right foot up his leg and into his hip socket.

He eyed the water bottle. He knew he ought to drink some, but he couldn't keep the water down. He never knew that pain could be so bad, it could make you want to throw up. And it wasn't getting better. If anything, it was getting worse.

Gradually, Nathan realized that he was chilled. That's when he noticed that it wasn't really light out anymore, which was crazy, because it was way too early to get dark. He looked up and swallowed hard as he saw a mass of dark gray clouds above him. A few minutes later he heard the first rumblings of thunder in the distance.

Don't think about Rich Morgan, Nathan told himself. *Chris is on the way down. He's got a CB in the truck. What happened to Rich is not going to happen to you.*

But a breeze picked up and he heard something beside him, something that sounded like a voice.

It can't be, Nathan told himself. *That's just the wind.*

Then he heard the noise again.

It has to be the wind, Nathan thought. The only problem was, the wind sounded just like a human voice. *That's impossible,* Nathan reasoned. *I know there's no one else on this ledge.*

Nathan tried to turn toward the voice and was rewarded with another searing blast of pain. Like the clouds above him, the pain kept building—getting denser, stronger, blocking out everything else. It wouldn't let him rest. The pain was going to burn him up, break him, eat him alive. It was going to drive him out of his mind.

Only one thing was stronger than the pain. The voice. The wind rose, and within it the voice grew louder, more insistent. Now Nathan could make out the words all too clearly. "No," a man's voice said. "Don't leave me up here alone. Please don't leave me alone."

As the afternoon passed, Nathan drifted in and out of consciousness. He kept hearing that voice. Worse, he could smell the odor of fear and old sweat mixed with a sickly-sweet stench—like something rotting. He didn't have any doubts now. There had to be someone else on the ledge with him.

"Who's there?" Nathan asked. "Where are you?"

For once, the voice didn't answer.

Then the smell got stronger, and the voice began again. Nathan could swear someone was whispering into his ear. He could feel breath on the back of his neck.

Down below, the coyotes sent up a round of their eerie cries. The sky grew even darker and then opened, as if the coyotes had called down the rain. A driving downpour began to spatter against the rock.

Nathan was shaking with cold now—wet, freezing, and writhing in pain. He knew that if Chris didn't get back soon, the rain would finish him off. The wind was going wild, as if it were trying to pry him off the rock. And within it, he still heard the voice, louder now, rising with the wind. "Don't leave me up here alone. Please don't leave me alone."

This is all in my mind, Nathan told himself. *I'm just hearing that voice 'cause I'm in pain and Chris told me that crazy ghost story. There's no one else up here. This is all my imagination.*

Lightning forked across the sky. And in its flash, Nathan saw the outstretched form of a man. He couldn't have been more than a few feet from him. His thin, cadaverous body was badly twisted. One leg had been splinted, and blood ran from his mouth. Bones jutted through his rotting flesh. But he turned his head toward Nathan and stretched out a pleading, blood-soaked hand.

The lightning faded and the sky went black again. Nathan felt the bloody hand touch his forehead, and then he didn't feel anything else.

"This way!" Chris shouted as he scrambled up one of the slabs, now slick from the storm. The wind was blowing hard, and the rain was whipping around in sheets. Behind Chris, four members of a Search and Rescue team struggled with a stretcher and medical supplies. A fifth member of the team remained down on the road with an ambulance, ready to take Nathan to the hospital.

Chris waited at the base of Abracadaver as the others caught up with him. "I couldn't find a fixed anchor when I came down off the ledge," he explained. "So I made my own. It should be okay for getting us back up one at a time."

But as Chris got ready to start up the rope something in the wind changed. Chris shook his head. It really sounded as if someone were screaming. *Is it Nathan?* he wondered. He listened, straining to separate the words from the wind. No, the voice was much deeper than his nephew's.

But as Chris started up the ropes, the ghostly voice became stronger—and Rich Morgan crept back into his thoughts. Rich Morgan's accident and Nathan's were a little too similar. And there was something unsettling about the fact that they had never found Rich's body. What if they couldn't find Nathan? What if there *was* something up there that wanted another climber dead?

*　　*　　*

Chris pulled himself over the lip and onto Lunch Ledge. For a moment, he just lay there, struggling to get his breath back. The rain was still coming down in torrents. The sky was black, the visibility zero. Chris clicked on his flashlight, terrified of what he'd find—or wouldn't find. "Nathan," he called out. "You still with us, bud?"

The voice that answered was much deeper than Nathan's. "Don't leave me up here alone. Please don't leave me here!"

"What the—" Chris stood up, scared now and furious with himself for everything that had gone wrong so far. He pushed his sodden hair out of his eyes and began searching. "Come on, Nathan," he called, "answer me!"

"Chris?" The voice was weak, but it was definitely Nathan's.

Chris rushed to his nephew's side and used his light to signal the search team. "How you doing?" he asked.

Nathan's face was drawn with pain. "I didn't think you'd come," he said. "I—I thought I'd have to stay up here with…with him."

"Who?" Chris demanded.

"Rich Morgan," Nathan said. "I saw his ghost, I swear. He—he touched me."

"Hey, it's okay," Chris said soothingly.

"He's lonely and he wants me to stay," Nathan insisted.

"Shhh—" Chris said. "You're going to be okay. I've got four guys from Search and Rescue right behind me."

Now Nathan was sobbing hysterically. "He's up here, Chris. You've got to listen to him. Someone's got to help him."

Chris held Nathan's good hand. "Okay, bud," he promised uselessly. "Whatever you want."

Chris hovered nervously as the medic examined Nathan. "If we can get him to the hospital tonight, he'll be okay," the medic finally announced. "We're going to splint him and get him onto the stretcher now."

While the Search and Rescue team worked on Nathan, Chris searched again for the anchors.

"Where are those things?" he muttered. Normally he could find the anchors on any route he climbed. But this night was definitely different.

A voice rose over the wind. "Over here!" it called.

Chris turned toward the voice and saw a light on the opposite side of the ledge. It didn't really make sense for the anchors to be over there, but he was ready to try anything. He headed toward the light, relieved that one of the rescue team had found the anchors.

"Over here!" the voice called again.

The light disappeared, but Chris had a good idea of where it had come from. He shone his own light over the area. Behind a scrub oak he saw the rusted heads of the anchors, just barely sticking out of a crack in the rock. He turned around, looking for the guy who'd signaled him. But there was only darkness and rain.

"Hey," Chris called out. "Where are you?"

In answer, one of the men carrying Nathan called out to him.

For the next three hours, Chris concentrated on getting Nathan down the rock and through the canyon.

It was only after Nathan was safely in the ambulance and Chris was sitting inside the Search and Rescue van with the rescue team that he remembered the voice on the ledge. One of the rescuers passed around a thermos of hot coffee. In a few minutes, Chris would get into his own truck and follow Nathan to the hospital, but now there was something he had to know.

"So who finally found the anchors?" Chris asked.

"Not me," said the medic who sat beside him. Two other rescue workers glanced up and shook their heads.

The fourth member of the team, an older man named Pablo, just sipped his coffee.

"Someone found the pitons," Chris said. "He called me over to them."

Pablo shrugged. "Maybe it wasn't one of us."

"What do you mean?" Chris asked.

"I mean there was a guy I used to climb with named Morgan. He died twenty years ago this weekend, right up on that ledge."

"Rich Morgan?" Chris asked.

Pablo nodded.

Chris sat perfectly still, remembering Nathan's hysterical babbling up on the ledge. He hadn't really believed it. He'd figured Nathan was out of his mind with pain. But now he had to wonder.

"You believe Rich's ghost was up on the ledge with us tonight?" Chris asked the older man.

"I believe he's the one who found those anchors," Pablo replied. "A dead man saved your nephew."

"Then the ghost story doesn't make sense," Chris said, desperate to find some logic in all of this. "Nathan said Rich was lonely," he continued. "That he wanted someone to stay up there with him. So if that's true, why'd he help us get him down?"

"Maybe because Nathan tried to help him," one of the men said. "He kept telling us we had to help Rich."

Pablo nodded. "Rich was a good guy. I reckon he thought your nephew deserved to live."

Chris shook himself, as if trying to wake from a bad dream. The wind was quiet now, and a stubborn part of him didn't want to believe that he, too, had heard Rich Morgan's pleading. "Just listen to us," he said wearily. "Talking about a ghost like it's real. You can believe anything when you're tired enough."

He opened the door of the van, ready to go back out. "Thanks for everything," he told the rescue team. "I never would have gotten Nathan down without you."

"You mean without *him*," Pablo said, nodding toward a light bobbing a short distance from the van.

"Did you see what I just saw?" asked the medic, his voice shaking.

"Let's get out of here," said one of the other rescue workers. "Now!"

Only Pablo didn't seem upset. "That's why Rich Morgan let Nathan come down," he said softly. "Rich came down with him."

Another flash of lightning split the sky, and Chris felt the hairs on the back of his neck rise. This time he, too, saw what was holding the light—and it wasn't a man. It was a figure made of twisted, bleached bones, a skeleton just barely held together by rotting, bloodied flesh.

THE WITCH CAT

June 4, 1848

Dear Sally,

Papa and I arrived here in Miles, North Carolina, late yesterday afternoon. Papa says Miles is "a sweet little town." I don't know about sweet, but it is sure is little. It's not even on the map! I think they called it Miles because it's miles from everything else on earth. Main Street, which is the town's <u>only</u> street, has a general store (which is also the post office), a tiny one-room schoolhouse, a barbershop, a church, and a newspaper office. The rest is all farmland.

Papa says he's fixing to buy us a plot of land here. I tried to tell him we need to live in a place where there are stores and theaters and concert halls. A place like Boston. But Papa says he's had enough of cities. He and Mama always planned to own some land in the country. Now that she's dead, he figures he's got to do what she would have wanted him to do.

Maybe I'm being foolish, but it scares me to be so far from everything. I took a walk yester-

day, just down Main Street, which is really a
narrow little road covered over with chestnut
trees. The trees got thicker and the road got darker the farther I walked. And I thought, a person
could vanish here and no one else would ever
know. So it looks as if I'm stuck in Miles, North
Carolina, miles from anywhere. I just wish I
didn't feel as if Papa made a terrible mistake
coming here. I've been having that funny feeling
along the back of my neck—the kind you
get when you know something awful is going to
happen and there's nothing you can do to stop it.

Please write and tell me how you are. I miss
you and I miss Boston.

Your very best friend,
Amanda

June 8, 1848

Dear Sally,
Papa's lost his heart to a piece of land here. It's a
three-acre parcel about ten miles out of town. For
some reason I don't like it, but I have to admit
it's pretty land. Most of it is flat and green.
Papa says it's rich soil, good for planting. The
north end of the property rises into rolling
hills. On the south end there's a wide, calm

pond edged by tall weeping willows.

Facing the pond is a small, broken-down house. No one's lived there for years. The roof leaks, the door is broken, the fireplace is falling apart, and the place is filthy. There's also an old barn, which isn't in much better shape.

Still, all Papa can talk about is the mountain laurel and bluebells growing wild in the woods, and what a beautiful home it's going to be for us. But something about those willow trees makes me uneasy. As though there were some real grief around that pond—as though something bad happened there a long time ago, and the land is still hurting over it.

And I got a real uncomfortable feeling when Papa asked Mr. Pierce, who runs the general store, about who owned the land.

"No one," Mr. Pierce answered.

"Then it's not for sale?" Papa said, sounding disappointed.

"It's yours if you want it," Mr. Pierce replied. He said that the land had once belonged to a family who left Miles because they had "a string of misfortunes." Made me think of a string of beads—like a necklace that brings you bad luck. Anyway, Mr. Pierce said he wouldn't

advise anyone to live there. He said something about how the place just wasn't _right_.

But you know how stubborn Papa can be. He said Miles is a small town, and small towns breed superstition. He didn't see anything wrong with that land, and he wasn't going to be scared off by local gossip. He says he's going to fix up that house, and we're going to have a good life there! I pray he's right and Mr. Pierce is wrong.

Papa says to send your parents his warmest regards.

Your very best friend,
Amanda

July 24, 1848

Dear Sally,

I'm sorry it's been so long since my last letter, but Papa and I have been very busy. Do you remember that land I told you about—the three acres with the pond? Well, we're living on it now. Since Papa didn't have to pay for the land, he hired some men to help us fix up the house and barn. I have a room of my own with blue gingham curtains. This week Papa's been building a chicken coop, and I've been planting an herb garden.

Every evening Papa says to me, "Well, we've

made it through another day without something terrible happening. Amanda, are you ready to give up all your silliness and admit that we're exactly where we ought to be?"

I'd like to, honestly I would. But the strangest thing happened the other day. It was just after dinner. Papa and I were sitting out on the front porch, watching the evening come in. The front of the cabin looks out on the pond. So we were sitting there, facing the water, when suddenly we saw a small skiff coming toward us. It was one of those little flat boats that a person stands on and then poles across the water. Anyway, the person on this skiff was a very beautiful woman. She had long tawny hair caught in a braid that hung down to her waist, and the greenest eyes I've ever seen.

She took the skiff up to our shore. Then she got off and walked right up to the house. She said her name was Caitlin O'Mara and she was our neighbor. She said she lives on the other side of the pond, and was glad to see that someone finally fixed this old place up.

Well, I think Papa's getting lonely out here. Especially with Mama gone. He was so glad for company that he invited her in for dessert. But

Caitlin O'Mara wouldn't take anything to eat. She said she had just wanted to meet us. And she stepped back onto that little skiff and poled her way back across the pond.

Sally, I'm feeling mean because I don't like Caitlin O'Mara, and I can see that Papa does. He couldn't take his eyes off her. I know he'll remarry one day, but I don't want it to be her. And I don't even know why. She was nice and polite as can be. But there's something about her I just don't trust. The minute she stepped onto our land I got that weird feeling—that something truly awful is about to happen.

Your very best friend,
Amanda

August 10, 1848

Dear Sally,

It's been two and a half weeks since Caitlin floated into our lives, but it feels like years. She's come by every day since then. Sometimes it's to bring Papa a pie she's made, or some beans from her garden. Today, she came by and gave me an old dress of hers, a pale yellow muslin. I suppose it's a fine enough dress—if you don't mind wearing something that's <u>hers</u>. Papa was standing

there, looking dazzled, as if Caitlin O'Mara
had just handed me the crown of England. I said
thanks, but Papa said I could be more gracious
than that.

But I can't be, Sally. Ever since that woman
started coming round, strange things have been
happening. When we first came to Miles, we
bought two dozen baby chicks, so we could have
our own eggs. Well, now six of those chicks are
dead. We don't know what's been getting them.
We just hear them screaming in the middle of the
night. And when we go out to the coops, we find
feathers and blood everywhere, and one or two
birds missing. Papa says it must be a fox, but I
don't know. I do know our chicks were just fine
before Miss Caitlin O'Mara started visiting.

And I've been having nightmares. Every
night I dream about a huge cat with tawny fur
and fiery green eyes. When the dream starts, I'm
in bed sleeping peacefully. But my window is
open. And as I'm sleeping, this big cat creeps in
through the window and curls up on the foot of
the bed. I feel it shift. First it moves against my
side. Then it gets up, and I feel its footsteps sinking into the bedclothes as it moves up to the head
of the bed. That's when I wake up screaming.

'Cause I know what that cat wants. It wants to rip my throat out.

I know this must all sound crazy to you: Poor Amanda moved to Miles and lost her mind. Sometimes that's how it feels to me, too. I'm so grateful I have a friend to tell about all this. There's no one I can talk to here. Please keep writing.

Your very best friend,
Amanda

August 31, 1848

Dear Sally,

Tomorrow's the first day of September. Already the nights are turning cool, and the leaves are starting to lose the deep green of summer. I guess I'm writing about the weather, because it's the only thing that feels safe to think about anymore.

We've lost more of the chicks. And yesterday morning I found a baby rabbit outside with its throat slashed.

Worse, Papa and I are not getting along. He keeps seeing more and more of that Caitlin woman. No matter how hard I try, I can't bring myself to like her. Papa says I'm a stubborn and

74

difficult girl. I can't help it, Sally. There's something about her that scares me. She shows up here every day now, but she's never once let us see her house. When Papa or I ask about it, she just goes on about how coming to visit us is such a lovely break in her day. And how her house is such a tiny place, without even a porch. Visiting with us is _so_ much nicer.

She kept asking why she never sees me wear her yellow dress. I finally lied and said it was too tight, when I'd never tried it on in my life. Papa made me try it on then and there. Wouldn't you know, the dress was too big! Caitlin was all for taking it in on the spot. But Papa was furious with me for lying and sent me to bed without supper. It was better than having a dress fitting with Caitlin!

The odd thing was, I only had her dress on for about three minutes, but it felt different from any muslin dress I've ever worn. The fabric clung to me as if it wasn't going to let go, as if it wanted to attach itself to my skin. It made me feel as though I was in the middle of one of those cat nightmares—which I still have every night. And the truth is, I've been feeling sickly ever since I put it on. Weakly and feverish. It's hard for me

75

to do a full day's work. Papa says I've just got a touch of the flu, and that I need more rest.

Write back soon, Sally. I miss you.

Your very best friend,
Amanda

September 5, 1848

Dear Sally,

I've pretty much been sick in bed ever since my last letter. But I was feeling better yesterday. And today Papa let me take the horse and wagon into town to get some supplies.

In the general store, Mr. Pierce asked me how Papa was doing, and I asked him what he knew about Caitlin O'Mara.

"You've seen her, then, have you?" he said, sounding only mildly surprised. "It's been a while since Caitlin has shown up in these parts." He gave me a strange look and said, "Probably fifty years or so. That's when the people who last had that land left Miles."

"What do you mean?" I said. "Caitlin couldn't have been here fifty years ago. She can't be a day older than thirty."

"Caitlin O'Mara's no ordinary woman," he told me. "She's a witch."

Sally, my whole body went cold when he said that.

"Then why do you let her stay here?" I asked. "Why don't you people run her out of town?"

"Because no one in their right mind wants to tangle with her," he answered. "They say she killed her husband years back. Did it with black magic."

I was shaking from the top of my head to the soles of my boots. "Well, what can we do?" I asked.

"Move," he told me. "Just leave that land like the people before you, and get as far away as you can."

"My papa won't do that," I said.

Mr. Pierce shrugged. "Well, if you can't get your daddy to leave, at least send him to see Old Alice."

Old Alice, it turns out, is what they call a "conjure woman." As far as I can tell, that means she's a witch, too, but the good kind, and the only one who can help us against Caitlin.

Oh, Sally, how am I ever going to get Papa to believe any of this? I don't even believe it! Good witches, bad witches—I'm beginning to think my

nightmares don't really end with the dawn. I
wish we'd never left Boston!

> Your very best friend,
> Amanda

October 13, 1848

Dear Sally,

I'm sorry to keep writing you with bad news.
After that day I went to town last month, I got
even sicker. High fever and chills, and the nightmares with me all the time. Papa said I was
delirious. Apparently, Caitlin kept trying to look
after me, but every time she crossed the doorway of
my room, I went into some sort of screaming fit.
This is what Papa tells me. I don't remember any
of it.

All I really remember is waking up in my
bed two days ago, feeling cool and smaller.
(Turns out I lost nearly twelve pounds!) Papa
was sitting beside me, muttering, "Oh, thank
you, thank you, thank you."

I looked up and saw a little white leather
pouch hanging over my bed. "What's that?" I
asked.

"Don't touch it," Papa said. "It's a protection."

I didn't know what he was talking about. Then Papa told me that when I was feverish, I kept telling him to go to Old Alice. Well, he finally went into town to try and get something to make me sleep, and he asked about Old Alice. Mr. Pierce sent Papa straight to her house. And she gave him this protection for me. It's got all sorts of strange things in it—feathers and dried grasses, bits of flowers, a bat's wing, and some blood from her fingertip. She told Papa to hang it over my bed. He said the minute he did, I calmed down and fell asleep. And ever since he put the pouch over my bed, I stopped screaming in my sleep.

I asked about Caitlin, if she was still coming by every day.

Papa just looked down and didn't answer for a while. Then he said, "We had an argument the day I hung that pouch over your bed. Caitlin saw it hanging there, and told me to take it down. She said I had no business exposing a young girl to such superstitious nonsense.

"I told her that as long as it helped you, that pouch was staying right where it was. She left then," Papa said. "And she hasn't come back." I could tell by his voice that he missed her, but he didn't say that.

"And what about the chickens?" I asked.

"We lost another four last night," he said in a quiet voice. "Something tore 'em apart. Didn't even bother to eat 'em. We're down to nine now."

I fell asleep then. When I woke up, a full day had passed. Papa was in my room, folding some of my dresses into a valise.

"What are you doing?" I asked him.

"Sending you away," he replied. Then he explained that he finally believed that something strange was going on. Whatever had been after the chickens got into the barn last night. He found our cow half-dead, with slash marks across her throat. "It will be back," he told me. "And this time I'll be waiting for it. With my knife."

"What's that got to do with me?" I asked.

"I don't want you here when it returns," Papa told me. "If it could take down a cow, I don't like to think of what it could do to you."

I begged and I pleaded. I even tried to prove I was too weak to travel. But Papa had made up his mind.

Early this afternoon he took me to Mrs. Crossen's house. This letter is being written at her kitchen table. Mrs. Crossen is the schoolmistress and a nice lady. She told me not to worry. She says everything will be fine. But I don't believe her. A wicked storm has been building all day. The wind has been howling and thunder's coming in over the hills. It's only four in the afternoon and already the sky is dark.

I'm scared, Sally. Papa shouldn't be out there alone, not tonight, not with whatever it is that's on that land. I tried to get Mrs. Crossen to take me back out there, but she says we'd never make it before the rain starts, and she's probably right.

I don't know if all our trouble has been caused by Caitlin O'Mara. But I do know I'm not crazy. There's something evil on that land, and it's trying to kill my papa.

> Your very best friend,
> Amanda

October 23, 1848

Dear Sally,

Once again I am writing to you from Mrs. Crossen's house. I won't be here long, though. I am coming back to Boston to live with my Aunt Hattie. This is because we buried Papa last week. I feel too sad to even write this down, but I can't keep all this sorrow to myself.

Do you remember how in my last letter I was worried about Papa being alone? Well, that night a terrible storm came up. The rain was coming down so hard it felt like needles on your skin. And the sky kept going white with lightning.

I couldn't stand the thought of Papa alone in the storm with whatever was attacking our animals. So I snuck out of Mrs. Crossen's house and took her horse, Blackie. Then I set off for our place. I didn't get more than a hundred yards before Blackie reared up, turned, and bolted straight back to his nice, dry barn. I can't say I blame him.

Mrs. Crossen found me in her barn, near-hysterical, trying to pull the poor horse back out into the storm again. She made me go back inside and said when the rain eased up she'd call on Mr. Griffith, one of her neighbors, and ask him to check on Papa.

So we sat in her kitchen and waited and waited. We watched the kerosene lamps burn and the hour grow late. It was after midnight when the wind finally died down and the rain let up. Just as she promised, Mrs. Crossen rode Blackie over to Mr. Griffith's farm, then came back and told me to get some sleep because everything was going to be all right.

But I didn't sleep. I couldn't. I knew nothing was going to be all right ever again.

Just before dawn Mr. Griffith knocked on Mrs. Crossen's door. He looked real sickly, and when she offered him some coffee and a muffin, he said it was going to be a while before he could eat anything.

Then he told us what had happened. He had gone over to our house. Papa wasn't in the house or in the barn or anywhere on the property. Instead, Mr. Griffith found him on the far shore of the pond. He was still alive then, although gravely injured. Mr. Griffith said he was bleeding something fierce, with deep gashes on his face and body. But he could still talk. And he told a very strange story, according to Mr. Griffith. Papa said something had been breaking into his barn and attacking his livestock. He'd waited for it that night all during the storm. Then exactly at midnight, a huge cat leapt through the barn window and attacked him. The same cat that was in my dreams, I'm sure of it. Anyway, Papa and the cat had a horrible fight, and Papa ended up cutting off the cat's right forepaw. Then he said the cat ran from the barn, and he followed it toward the pond. There he saw a mark in the mud, where a skiff had been pushed from the shoreline into the water. So Papa took his own boat and went after the skiff.

That's all Papa got to say. According to Mr. Griffith, after Papa told him about rowing across the lake, he just closed his eyes and didn't wake up again. He died one hour later in Doc Taylor's office.

Doc Taylor still won't tell me what killed Papa. He doesn't have to. Mr. Griffith said that when they found Papa he was holding on to the severed paw of a giant cat. And just a few yards from him lay Caitlin O'Mara. She was dead, and her right hand was missing.

I can't write about this anymore, Sally. It still feels like a knife going through me when I think about Papa dying. I'll see you soon, though. I wish I could say I was happy about that. But I can't help thinking that Caitlin O'Mara is the one responsible for me coming back to Boston—without my papa.

Your very best friend,
Amanda

PLANET GROSS

"This is so sick!" Ben cried out in delight. "I'm telling you, Tor, these graphics are extreme!"

Tori Barnes slammed shut the door of her room, so she wouldn't have to listen to her brother exclaim about his latest video game. She was tired of video games, CD-ROM players, modems, nets, and everything else related to computers. She wouldn't care if she never saw another computer again. Unfortunately, the chances of that weren't too likely, since she lived in the House of Nerds.

Ben and Tori's dad, a university professor, taught graduate courses in artificial intelligence. Their mother was an internationally known software consultant with a home office that featured the most advanced computer technology. Tori's older brother, John, was at MIT, following in their parents' footsteps. And her geeky thirteen-year-old brother, Ben, was a video-game junkie.

The computer on Tori's desk beeped. She sighed and went to look at the screen. Sure enough, there was an E-mail message from Ben:

The new game, Planet Gross, is the ultimate! I dare you to play, nano-brain!

That was the other thing about Ben. He was convinced that if you weren't as obsessed with computers as he was, you were an idiot. Tori knew she wasn't an idiot. She just wasn't into computers the way the rest of her family was.

Actually, she was interested in different things altogether. Tori took down a book from her shelf, curled up on her bed, and began to read. Lately, she'd become intrigued by magic. She'd been reading everything she could find in the library and now knew a smattering about ancient Egyptian magic, Celtic magic, voodoo, and some contemporary forms of witchcraft. She wasn't sure that she really believed in any of it, but it was definitely more exciting than another stupid computer game.

The door to Tori's bedroom opened and Ben barged in. "I challenged you to a game of Planet Gross," he announced.

"I don't care," Tori replied. "I'm reading."

"You're a wimp," Ben said.

"And you're a squeeb," Tori said.

Mrs. Barnes poked her head through the

doorway. "Don't you two have anything better to do than insult each other?" she asked.

"I was just asking Tori if she'd play my new video game with me," Ben said in an innocent voice.

"Tori?" her mother asked.

"I'm reading," Tori said, hoping her mother wouldn't notice the title of the book. She knew her mom didn't approve of anything connected with magic.

"The book will wait, Tori," Mrs. Barnes said. "Why don't you just spend ten minutes with your brother?" Lately Mrs. Barnes had become concerned that the members of her family were drifting apart. For the last month, she'd been trying to get all three of her kids to spend time together. She'd even flown John down from MIT for a family picnic.

"All right," Tori said. She knew it would be useless to argue with her mom. "Ten minutes. But that's it!"

Tori followed Ben into his room and watched as he started up the new game. "See, there are two scientists exploring Planet Gross," Ben explained. "Dr. Rupert DeLong and Dr. Viola May. We'll start with Dr. May."

Tori watched listlessly as yet another tiny video character bopped up and down on a computer landscape. This one was more realistic than most of them, Tori had to admit. The scientist looked like a real person, not like a cartoon. For a moment Tori wondered if she were a real actress whose image had been reduced by computer.

Dr. Viola May ducked into caves, shot down waterfalls, and fell into sandpits, only to pop right out again.

"So what's the big deal?" Tori asked. "This looks like every other game you play."

"Watch," Ben said. "This is just the opening level. She hasn't met any of the planet's monsters yet."

"I can't wait," Tori murmured.

Ben entered a code, and soon Dr. May was bopping through the next level of the game. Suddenly Tori understood why Ben loved this game so much.

Every few seconds, one of the planet's monsters would jump out. If Dr. May wasn't quick enough, the creature would zap her—with disgusting results.

"Yuck!" Tori yelled as Dr. May's forehead

exploded, sending millions of white worms slithering across the screen.

"No biggie," Ben said.

Tori watched in disbelief as the tiny scientist pieced her forehead back together and traveled on. A few seconds later, an enormous blue sloth zapped her with a ray from its forehead. This time Dr. Viola May stood perfectly still as each of her fingers dropped to the ground, leaving stumps gushing deep red blood. It all looked appallingly real.

"This is extremely sick," Tori told Ben. "I'm out of here."

"What's the matter?" Ben taunted. "Can't take it?"

"Oh, please," Tori said. "I can take anything you can."

"Then watch one more," Ben dared her.

Tori crossed her arms over her chest and looked bored. "Fine. One more, dweeb."

This time, Dr. Viola May peered into a hole on the surface of the planet. Seconds later, small green batlike creatures rose out of the hole and attached themselves to her body. The video zoomed in to a close-up on the bat things. They made loud sucking sounds as they munched on the scientist's flesh. Next came a close-up of Dr. May—her face frozen in a mask of terror as green slime oozed out of her eyes, ears, and nose. A bat-thing swooped down to suck the green gunk up.

Tori thought she was going to be sick. She bolted from Ben's room, heading straight for the bathroom. Her brother's laughter followed her down the hallway.

Moments later she leaned against the bath-room wall, waiting for the wave of nausea to pass. That game was the grossest thing she'd ever seen. She wondered if her parents knew just where Ben's computer obsessions were taking him. She couldn't talk to her mother about it. Mrs. Barnes had already left for a lecture she was giving this evening. But her dad would be home soon. Maybe he would listen.

Tori waited until dinner was over and her father had retreated to his study. Mr. Barnes sat behind his desk, sorting through the mountain of paper that covered it. For such a precise math-ematical type, he was a mess. "Hey, Tor," he said as she entered. "What's up?"

"I need to talk to you about Ben," Tori

began. "Have you seen his latest video game, Planet Gross?"

Her father gave her a weary look. "Tor, I've barely had time to read my students' term papers. No, I haven't been checking out your brother's computer games."

"Well, maybe you should," Tori said. "This one is disgusting. It's the sickest thing I've ever seen. It's violent and gross and—"

"Slow down," her father said. "Now, I know you don't like Ben's games, but I really think it's because you're avoiding your own competitive spirit."

"I am not!" Tori protested.

But her father wasn't listening. "If you want Ben to stop bothering you, then you've got to learn to beat him at his own game." Mr. Barnes gave Tori a reassuring wink. "You know what your name means, Victoria—*victory!*"

"Thanks a lot, Dad," Tori muttered as she left the study.

Tori decided that she'd just have to do her best to avoid Ben until some new video game caught his attention. But ignoring Ben wasn't easy. He was becoming totally obsessed with

Planet Gross as he progressed through higher and higher levels of the game. He played every day before and after school. And he kept trying to get Tori to play.

The more Tori resisted, the more determined Ben became. One day he caught her reading one of her magic books. He plucked the book from her hand. "Witchcraft, Tor?" he said. "I bet Mom would love to hear that you're messing with witchcraft. You know how she feels about stuff like that."

Tori did know. She'd be grounded for the rest of her life.

Ben gave Tori a smarmy smile. "I'll make you a deal," he said. "I won't say a word to Mom if you just agree to play a few games..."

From then on, Tori had no choice but to play Planet Gross whenever Ben felt like torturing her. It was either that, or he would tell on her.

Even when Tori wasn't playing Planet Gross, she couldn't escape it. Ben couldn't seem to play silently. His shouts boomed down the hallway and into her room: "Oh, gross! Supersick! Eeeww—he's spewing vomit! Ugh! I can't believe he's hurling, and it looks so real—he must have eaten a pizza!"

Tori was so sick of Planet Gross she thought she'd go crazy. She kept her door closed and bought earplugs. For a while it was okay. But Ben found a way to get to her. Tori came home from school one day and booted up her computer. Instead of the usual opening messages, Tori was greeted by two of the oozing monsters from Planet Gross.

"Tori Barnes," said one of the disgusting little creatures, "you are too stupid to enter our universe. Therefore, we have been forced to enter yours."

As Tori watched, stunned, the first monster plucked out the second's eyeball and ate it. The second zapped the first with a ray, and the first creature's stomach opened and all its guts spilled toward the bottom of the screen.

Tori was about to shut off the computer when the sickening fight suddenly stopped. It was followed by a message from Ben, explaining how he had managed to reproduce the graphics from the game and transfer them onto her computer. It ended with one of Ben's typical snarky digs: "Bet you couldn't do that, could you? And by the way, lamebrain, you really shouldn't keep your diary on your hard drive. I can't believe you *kissed* Robbie Greer. Talk about gross!"

With a shriek, Tori raced into Ben's room. "Keep off my machine!" she screamed loudly. Then she realized that she was shouting at an empty room. Ben wasn't there.

Feeling slightly silly, she went down to the kitchen, where her father was making a salad. "Do you know where Ben is?" she asked.

"He went to that CD-ROM exhibition," her father said. "Didn't you want to go to that too?"

"Not exactly," Tori said. But when her father gave her a disappointed look, she went on. "I mean, I'd love to but I've got to study for a test."

Her father nodded and Tori returned to her room. Determined to undo Ben's damage, she went to her computer, found the program Ben had added to it, and erased it from her hard drive. She transferred her diary to a disk and put it in the back of her desk drawer. Then she sat staring at the screen, wondering how to put a stop to her brother.

Tori looked at one of the books about magic on her bed, and she thought about what her dad had said—all that stuff about being competitive and beating Ben at his own game. The truth was that even though Tori wasn't as computer-mad as the rest of her family, she'd grown up living and breathing bytes like everyone else in the house. For a twelve-year-old, she knew an awful lot about computers, and so when she thought up a rather complex plan, she was pretty sure she could pull it off.

First Tori marched into Ben's room and removed the game cartridge for Planet Gross. *It's a good thing Mom's at a business conference this week,* Tori thought as she headed for her mother's office. There she surveyed the bank of state-of-the-art computers, CD-ROM players, and video components. Then she did something that even Ben had never done. She got into the game software and began to alter the graphics.

Three hours later, Tori took the altered game up to her room. There was one last part to her plan, and this was the part she wasn't sure of. Still, she knew she had to try and do it quickly. Ben was supposed to leave the next day for two weeks at a school-sponsored computer camp.

In the darkened room, Tori lit two candles. Between them she placed a photograph of Ben, and then she began to work magic....

The next two weeks were the best of Tori's life. As far as Mr. and Mrs. Barnes knew, Ben was at computer camp. Only Tori knew where he really was—and that was a long way from camp.

It wasn't often that Tori missed her brother, but when she did—as she did right now—she just whipped out her Planet Gross game and turned it on.

Tori sat back against the pillows on her bed and watched calmly as a tiny Dr. Ben Barnes turned to face her.

"Come on, Tor!" he said furiously. "You've got to get me out of here! I want *off* this planet!"

"I'll release you eventually," Tori promised in a comforting tone. "But not yet, Ben. Now we've got a game to play. You know," she told him, "it's a shame you can't watch this. The graphics are excellent!"

Tori punched in the code for the second level of the game and watched as Dr. Barnes got zapped by a ray from one of the planet's grossest monsters. Nanoseconds later, Dr. Barnes screamed with horror as tiny snakes burst from his skin and sank their fangs back into his flesh.

Tori didn't even need to watch his little body turn black and bloated. She exited the game with a contented sigh. "Victory," she murmured.

THE WOMAN IN WHITE

Claudia Olmedos led the way across a wide sandy wash. Behind her were her fourteen-year-old sister Rosa and Jill Hander, who had just moved to the Southwest from New York. "So what do you think of the desert?" Claudia asked Jill.

"This place is like another planet compared to where I come from," Jill answered. "This big sky and these mountains and all this cactus—"

"We should have gone to the mall," Rosa broke in irritably. Rosa, who was a year and a half older than Claudia, had been really moody lately.

Rosa's eyes followed Jill, who was now walking ahead of them. "I wouldn't wander off if I were you," she warned. "City people are always getting themselves killed out here."

Jill gave Rosa a startled look. "You don't like the desert much, do you?"

"It's got nothing to do with like or dislike," Rosa answered. "I don't trust it. I feel like the desert is always waiting for me to make a mis-

97

take. Just one mistake—I don't carry enough water or I miss the trail or I step too close to a rattler. That's all it takes. It's just waiting to get me and you and anyone else who makes a mistake."

Jill shrugged apologetically. "My little brother, Malcolm, and I—we're always wandering off. It must run in the family or something."

"Well, don't do that here," Rosa said, a little more gently. "It's not only snakes and scorpions that are dangerous. There are other things in the desert, really scary things that most people won't even talk about—"

Claudia glared at her sister. "Will you shut up? What are you—the voice of doom?"

Jill came to an abrupt halt. "I think I just found a canyon," she said in an awed voice. About two feet from where she stood, the desert floor suddenly dropped twenty feet straight down.

"That's an arroyo," Claudia explained with a smile. "But we call them canyons too. It's actually a water course. When it rains, the water cuts through the sandy soil and forms channels. During a rain, an arroyo can flood in about two minutes."

Jill stared at the sandy channel. "Cool. Can we can go down there?"

"Sure," Claudia answered.

Rosa folded her arms over her chest. "Claudia, have you lost your mind?" she demanded. "You know better than to go into an arroyo during monsoon season. Are you trying to get caught in a flash flood?"

"Oh, Rosa—" Claudia began.

"The wind is up," Rosa added. "Listen."

The three girls stood still. Claudia could hear the familiar sound of the wind moving across the desert floor. Sometimes the wind was so clear she could swear she heard it parting the branches of mesquite trees, lifting tumbleweeds into the air, and bringing rain from across the mountains. And sometimes she felt as if she heard the things—coyotes calling, jets streaking across the sky, voices—caught inside it.

"Come on," Rosa said impatiently, starting back through the tangle of mesquite and paloverde trees. "Before *La Llorona* gets us."

"Who?" Jill asked.

"Rosa, don't start," Claudia pleaded.

"Start what?" Jill asked. "What's this 'la yarona'?"

Claudia sighed, knowing there was no way out of the explanation. "It's *llorona*," she said. "In Spanish, the double *l* is pronounced like a *y*. So it's pronounced *la ya-rona*. It means 'The Weeping Woman' or 'The Wailing One.'"

"Who is she?" Jill asked.

"It's just a superstition," Claudia said. For as long as Claudia could remember, her mother had tried to scare her and Rosa with stories of *La Llorona*. Claudia thought the old folktale was dumb. It had only made her determined never to scare her kids or anyone else with such ridiculous stories.

Rosa, however, liked scary stories. "*La Llorona* was a woman who lived a long time ago," she began as they headed back to the adobe houses that bordered the desert. "The story goes that she was a beautiful young peasant woman named Maria. One day a rich young man, a *ranchero,* rode into her village and fell in love with her. They were married, but his family would never approve of his marrying someone so poor, so he never told them. He lived with Maria in her little *casita* by the river, and they had three children."

"This is a total soap opera," Claudia warned.

"Let me finish," Rosa said. "One day the young man rides off. He doesn't tell Maria, but he's going home to visit his family. And once he's there, his family insists that he take a proper wife from his own class. Being a major wimp, he agrees, and then he does a *really* dumb thing. He goes back to the village and tells Maria he's got to marry this other woman."

"He's scum," Jill decided.

"That's what Maria thought, too," Rosa said. "She was furious, and told him to leave. But she was also curious. She couldn't help herself. She went to the wedding."

Claudia sighed loudly. "I told you it was a soap opera," she said.

Rosa's voice became hushed and dramatic as she continued the tale. "So there's Maria, standing in the back of the church, watching the love of her life marry this rich woman. And she just goes crazy. Stark raving insane. She runs home, kills all her kids, throws their bodies in the river, and then drowns herself."

"Lovely," Jill murmured.

"There's more," Rosa went on. "After Maria dies, her soul tries to get into heaven. But the angel or whoever's up there asks her, 'Where are your children?' And she says she doesn't know. The angel tells her that she has to find them and bring them there—and that she can't rest until she does. So ever since, she's been wandering around rivers and streams and washes, weeping and wailing as she searches for her kids. They say she wears the white shroud she was buried in."

"So she's like a local ghost?" Jill asked.

Rosa nodded. "Exactly. The legend says that when she can't find her own children, *La Llorona* takes *other* children."

Jill knelt to retie her sneaker. "Takes them where?"

"No one knows," Rosa said mysteriously. "But when it rains and *La Llorona* walks the desert, children just vanish. No one ever finds them. It's been going on for centuries."

"Oh, stop it, Rosa!" Claudia said as she saw Jill looking frightened. "It's a story, like the boogeyman. Adults tell it so kids will listen when they're told not to play in the washes." She softened her tone as she explained. "My mother had me terrified of *La Llorona* for years—it's just an old story."

"Is it?" Jill asked in a quiet voice.

"Of course it is," Claudia said.

Two weeks later, Claudia and Rosa went to a slumber party at Jill's house. Jill's parents were watching TV in their room, leaving the rest of the house to Jill and her friends.

The five girls at the sleepover ordered in pizza, watched videos, and spent an hour dissing all the boys in the neighborhood.

"Now what?" Jill asked at nine-thirty. "It's too early to go to sleep."

"Let's have a séance!" said a red-haired girl named Nicole. "You know, we turn off the lights and all sit around a table holding hands. Then we try to contact a spirit." She nodded toward the windows. "It just started raining. It's perfect spooky weather."

The girls arranged themselves around the Handers' dining room table. They turned out the lights and linked hands. Outside, the wind rose and rain pounded against the windows. But the séance was a bust. The only thing they managed to "call up" was Jill's little brother Malcolm, who wandered into the room looking for his stuffed rabbit.

"Let's try something else," said Nicole after

Mr. Hander had put Malcolm to bed. "I heard that if you stare into a mirror by candlelight and say the name of a dead person forty-seven times, you'll see their face in the mirror instead of your own."

"Then what?" Claudia asked.

Nicole shrugged. "It's sort of an invitation to the spirit, to come from their world into ours. Then it can hang out in this world as long as it wants."

"I'll go first," said Loreen, a thin blond girl.

"Okay, let's try it in the bathroom," Jill decided. "That's got the biggest mirror."

The girls trooped into the bathroom. Jill lit a candle and shut off the lights.

Loreen stared into the darkened mirror. Finally, she began in a whispery voice, "Zoe, Zoe, Zoe, Zoe..."

"I can't believe this!" Nicole interrupted. "She's trying to call up the spirit of her dead dog!"

"I loved Zoe!" Loreen said in a hurt tone.

"It has to be a *human* spirit," Nicole said.

"I've got it!" Rosa said. She looked at Claudia. "I'm going to call up Grandma."

Claudia groaned. "Well, if you do, she's only

going to ask us if we brushed our teeth today. That's all she used to say, remember?"

"I'm going to try anyway," Rosa said. She stared into the mirror and intoned their grandmother's name until Claudia thought she'd die of boredom.

Nothing happened.

"Let's try a dead rock star," Jill suggested. She, too, chanted a name forty-seven times. "All I see is me," Jill finally said in a disappointed tone.

"That's because this doesn't work," Claudia said. "Why don't we all go watch some more videos?"

The other girls started to agree with her until Rosa said, "Wait a minute. Maybe we need the kind of spirit that's already walking around. Come on, Claudia, it's your turn. Do *La Llorona*."

Claudia felt a chill go through her at the suggestion. "No way," she said. "This whole idea is crazy."

"You don't believe in her anyway," Rosa reminded her. "So what's the problem?"

"Come on, Claudia," Loreen said. "Just try. Everyone else has."

Claudia looked at Jill, and for a moment she was sure she saw fear in Jill's eyes. But Jill shrugged and said, "Give it a shot."

Claudia stood in front of the candlelit mirror. The others were gathered behind her, staring into the dark reflection. Claudia giggled nervously and felt Rosa poke her in the ribs. "I can't help it," she said. "I feel silly."

"Just do it," Rosa snapped.

"Okay," Claudia said. "*La Llorona, La Llorona, La Llorona...*"

She didn't know how many times she said the name. She just said it over and over, figuring that when she'd said it a bunch of times, she'd quit and no one would know the difference.

Suddenly Claudia's voice stuck in her throat. A face was staring back at her from the mirror: a woman's face, gaunt and terrifying. A tattered white shroud covered the woman's head and shoulders. Claudia could see that she had once been very beautiful. She had high cheekbones, dark hair, and big, dark eyes. But now her skin was mottled, her lips were black, and an eerie red flame flickered in her pupils. Claudia felt her own skin crawl. Looking at *La Llorona* was like looking at the face of death.

"Claudia? Claudia, what's wrong?" Rosa asked sharply.

Unable to speak, Claudia pointed to the mirror.

"What is it?" Nicole asked.

"Don't you see her?" Claudia asked, her throat raw.

"See who?" Loreen asked. "You?"

Claudia stared. The woman was still there, fixing her with a steady, burning gaze, as if memorizing Claudia's face for all time. Then the woman raised a hand to her tear-stained cheek, and Claudia saw long, gleaming fingernails.

The figure in the mirror spoke in a rasping whisper, "You. You called me. Now you'll give me one of my children."

Panicked, Claudia grabbed her sister's arm.

"*La Llorona*. Sh—she just spoke," Claudia stammered. "Didn't you hear her?"

"Very funny," Loreen said.

"But not convincing," Rosa added.

Jill's mother rattled the doorknob and called through the closed door: "Why are all five of you locked in the bathroom?"

"It's all right, Ma," Jill called back. "We're coming out now."

Jill switched on the bathroom lights, and the image of *La Llorona* disappeared. Claudia was relieved to see her own reflection reapppear in the mirror. She stood for a moment, reassured by the sight of her own features. Behind her, the other girls filed out of the bathroom, talking about which video to watch.

No one else had seen the hideous face in the mirror, Claudia realized. She was the only one who knew she'd actually called up *La Llorona*.

That night, Claudia couldn't get to sleep. Thunder crashed and white-hot lightning split the sky. The wind howled, whipping around the house and pushing against the windows as if it wanted to get inside.

Claudia lay in her sleeping bag, watching the storm through the Handers' living room window. The wind was louder than she'd ever heard it. If you let your imagination get carried away, she thought, you could almost believe it wasn't wind at all, but a woman wailing.

On the other side of the room, Rosa turned over and sighed. "*La Llorona*," she said softly.

All the next day, the rain continued to fall. Mrs. Olmedos put Claudia and Rosa to work making tortillas in the kitchen. Claudia had always loved their family cooking days. Her mother would play Mexican music on the tape deck and tell the girls stories from her childhood. But today, Claudia had no patience for making tortillas or listening to stories. She felt as if she were going crazy. Something bad was going to happen. She could feel it in her bones. It was going to be something really awful. She was the only one who knew about it, and there was nothing she could do to stop it.

Claudia woke early the next morning. It was just past six. The rain had stopped, leaving a cool, overcast sky, heavy with clouds. Claudia thought about going back to sleep, but knew it was useless. She still had that awful feeling she'd had ever since the night of Jill's party.

She dressed quietly, careful not to wake Rosa, and went into the kitchen where she made herself breakfast. She scanned the morning paper and was relieved not to find any accounts of disaster. Nothing terrible had happened. Maybe she was wrong.

The restlessness was still with her, though. She didn't know where she wanted to go or what she wanted to do, but she couldn't stay inside. She got on her mountain bike and began riding.

Claudia began riding from the streets and houses and headed toward the desert.

She rode east until she came to the last paved road. Moments later, she was following a narrow trail that wound through mesquite, ironwood, and acacia trees. She took a deep breath, inhaling the sweet, musky scent that the creosote bushes gave off when the ground was wet. The desert was especially beautiful under cloudy skies. The greens of the cactus and trees were more intense. Everything seemed clearer. Without the glare of the sun, the desert seemed to reveal its true nature.

The sick feeling suddenly came back to her as she looked up. Vultures were circling in the distance. Inside her, a voice whispered, "*La Llorona*."

That's crazy, Claudia told herself. Besides, if it was *La Llorona*, she wouldn't have left a body, would she? It was probably a dead jackrabbit.

Claudia rode toward where the large birds were circling. But by the time she'd reached the spot where she thought they were, they'd gone—probably in search of other carrion. She got off her bike and looked around, but she couldn't find anything except the usual cactus and lizards. She noticed, though, that she was near the arroyo—the same one she'd seen with Rosa and Jill.

Claudia knew it was stupid to go into a wash after a storm. There could be more runoff from the mountains, and there was a chance that she might be caught in a flash flood. Still, she felt irresistibly drawn into the arroyo.

She leaned her bike against a mesquite tree and dropped down into the wash. Steep walls of gray-brown sand rose on either side of her. Beneath her feet, the damp ground was covered with the pebbles, sticks, and roots that had been carried downstream by the rains.

Claudia began to wander upstream, noting the usual signs of rain—the pools of shallow water and the piles of debris caught on the sides of the arroyo.

The arroyo became narrower and deeper, its edges pocketed with caves. They weren't real caves, just deep crevices in the sand walls hollowed out by water. When she and Rosa were young, they used to hide out inside caves just like these. Then one day, their mother caught them. Claudia still remembered the scathing lecture and her mother's vivid demonstration of how dangerous the caves were. She'd pulled the two girls out of the cave, then pressed her hand against one of its sand walls. Seconds later, the entire cave collapsed.

Claudia kept walking, unsure of what she was looking for. And then she found it: the small footprints of a child pressed into the damp sand.

Claudia's heart began to pound. As she followed the tracks upstream, she was barely aware of the wind rising or of the chorus of coyotes. She was listening for something else. For the sound of a woman weeping for her dead children.

What Claudia actually heard was a child's voice. It was definitely a little boy, somewhere up around the next bend. And his voice sounded familiar.

"No," he was crying. "I don't *want* to go with you! Let go of me!"

Where do I know that voice from? Claudia asked herself. And then she remembered little Malcolm wandering into the séance, looking for his stuffed rabbit.

"Stop!" Claudia screamed as she raced forward. "Leave him alone!"

The child's next words terrified her. He was sobbing now. "Please don't scratch me. Your nails hurt. Please don't scratch me!"

Claudia rounded the bend in the wash and faced a horrible sight: Jill's brother, Malcolm, was struggling in the grasp of the woman in white. The spirit *she* had called up.

Claudia reached out and grabbed one of Malcolm's hands. "Stop!" she cried. "Let him go!"

La Llorona turned to glare at her. The red flames flickered in her eyes. She smiled at Claudia with teeth as sharp as the long curving nails on her fingers. "*Gracias,*" she said. "You gave me my child."

"He's not yours, and I didn't give him to you!"

"Ah, but you did," *La Llorona* replied. "You called me. Consider this your answer."

In the next instant, *La Llorona*'s hand flashed out and raked five deep gouges in Claudia's right arm. Claudia screamed in pain, and her left hand flew up to cradle her arm. Blood welled from the cuts, and strips of skin hung from the wound. She couldn't believe how much it hurt. It felt as though she'd been sliced open by five razors. Claudia stared at her bloodied arm and tried not to gag.

Malcolm began to scream in terror.

Malcolm! Claudia thought. *I let go of his hand!*

Frantically, she reached for the boy. But it was too late. *La Llorona* had yanked him into one of the caves.

"No!" Claudia cried, racing after them.

She was less than ten feet from the cave when the sky opened again and torrents of rain poured down.

"No!" Claudia screamed again as a wall of sand collapsed across the entrance to the cave. "Malcolm!" she called. "Malcolm, where are you?"

Soaking wet and shivering, Claudia began digging through the mountain of wet earth that covered Malcolm Hander.

Claudia never knew how long she dug—it felt like hours. She dug until her mother and a group of neighbors found her, knee-deep in the rushing current, crying hysterically and weak from loss of blood.

She didn't remember much after that. She knew she told them about *La Llorona* and Malcolm. She knew they promised to keep searching. But all that was left of the cave was swept away by the rains.

The five cuts on Claudia's arm healed. They left long, jagged white scars that twinged a little whenever it rained. But Claudia could hardly complain about her scars—not when she had to live with the fact that no trace of Malcolm had ever been found.

And there was one more thing that haunted Claudia, something that didn't happen often, but never went away. Every now and then, Claudia would glance quickly at her reflection in a mirror or a store window. And staring back at her would be the gruesome face of the woman in white.

KILLER BEES

Jeremy Hughes sat absolutely still as a large brown tarantula climbed up his bare arm, making its way toward his shoulder. Sheldon, the tarantula, liked to hang out at exactly the point where Jeremy's shoulder and neck met. Especially since Gertrude, a red-kneed tarantula, had disappeared about a week ago. Even though the two tarantulas had lived in separate aquariums, Jeremy was convinced that Sheldon was lonely now.

Jeremy heard a knock on his bedroom door. Then the door opened and his mother walked in. She gave her son a pained look. "How do you know that spider won't take a bite out of your neck?" she asked.

"Because Sheldon's a tarantula, not a vampire," Jeremy explained. "He's my pet, Mom. He doesn't bite unless he feels threatened, and he knows I'm his friend."

"Well, I'm here to talk to you about one of your human friends," his mother said. "Eric—"

"Eric Thompson is not my friend," Jeremy

cut her off. "He may be your best friend's son, but there's no way—"

"Jeremy, I'm not going to argue with you," his mother said. "Eric's sitter just canceled, so he's coming over tonight while Anne and I are out. You two don't have to play together. But I expect you to be civil."

Jeremy rolled his eyes. He and Eric had been thrown together all their lives, and they'd never gotten along. Not even for a day. That was because Eric was a bully and a moron. Jeremy decided he'd just stay upstairs in his room. Eric could stay downstairs with the TV and Casey, the babysitter. Casey was cool, Jeremy reminded himself. She'd keep Eric from tearing the house apart.

Within a half hour both Casey and Eric had arrived, and Jeremy could tell that it was not going to be a good night.

"I'm eleven!" Eric said loudly as his mother pushed him through the Hugheses' front door. "I don't need a sitter!" Eric was tall for a fifth grader, about six inches taller than Jeremy. He had thick brown hair, freckles across the bridge of his nose, and mean, close-set eyes.

"Be good, honey," his mother said, giving him a kiss. "We'll be back soon."

"Make sure you listen to Casey," Jeremy's mother called out.

But Casey was in rough shape. Her eyes were red and puffy, and she kept sniffing loudly.

"You got a cold?" Eric asked her.

Casey shook her head. "My boyfriend just broke up with me," she explained. "I've got to call Laura." Laura, Jeremy knew, was Casey's best friend.

Casey headed straight for the phone. Seconds later she was talking intensely. It was clear that she was not going to be keeping an eye on Eric.

Eric punched Jeremy in the arm. "So, dweeb. What are we doing tonight?"

"I've got homework," Jeremy answered.

"You are such a dork—" Eric began.

"But my mom rented all these videos," Jeremy went on quickly. "They're by the TV."

Eric went to check out the videos and Jeremy escaped to his room. He shut the door with a sigh of relief. Downstairs he heard the TV blaring.

For a while the videos kept Eric busy, and Jeremy concentrated on his bug collection. He wanted to be an entomologist when he grew up, and his room was proof. He had an ant farm, two tarantula tanks, a praying mantis cocoon, an empty beehive, a ladybug colony, a butterfly collection, and every book on bugs that he could get his hands on. After feeding Sheldon some grubworms, Jeremy curled up with his latest book, one on Africanized honeybees, and began reading.

An hour later the door to Jeremy's room flew open and Eric stomped in. "I'm bored," he declared. "Those videos are totally lame."

All these years, Jeremy had managed to keep Eric out of his room. Now he was sure Eric was going to damage something. He had to get him out. "Why don't we go downstairs and play a game?" Jeremy offered.

"No, let's stay up here," Eric said. He headed straight for the ant farm and lifted it into the air. "What happens if I drop this?" he wondered aloud.

"Put it down," Jeremy ordered.

Eric put down the ant farm but knelt by the tarantula tank and leered at Sheldon. "That's the most disgusting thing I've ever seen," he said. "A giant hairy spider. Is it poisonous?"

"Only a little," Jeremy said truthfully. "Tarantulas have venom, but it's not like a black widow's or a brown recluse spider's—it won't kill you."

"I thought you had two of these things," Eric said idly.

"Yeah. Gertrude disappeared about a week ago," Jeremy said. "I've looked for her everywhere. She must have gotten outside somehow."

But Eric wasn't listening. He was staring at a map of the Americas pinned to Jeremy's wall.

"How come there are all these colored zones in South and Central America?" Eric asked. "And how come they're dated?"

Jeremy decided that explaining a map was safer than letting Eric get too interested in Sheldon. He went over to the map and pointed to Brazil, where the year 1957 had been inked in. "This is a map of the spread of the Africanized honeybee," Jeremy explained.

"You mean killer bees?"

"That's what some people call them," Jeremy admitted. "But it's not because they're psychopaths or anything. It's just that they're more aggressive than the European honeybees. If they think someone is threatening their hive, a lot of them may attack at once."

"How much is a lot?" Eric asked.

"Well," Jeremy said, thinking back to an article he'd read. "They killed a dog last year—it had three thousand bee stings in its head." Jeremy pointed to the map. "See, they were first brought from Africa to Brazil in 1956. But they escaped in 1957 and started spreading north. By 1975 they were in Suriname; Colombia in 1980; Costa Rica in 1983—"

"So what?" Eric interrupted. "Who cares where a bunch of bees were back in the eighties?"

"How about where they are now?" Jeremy asked.

Once again, Eric had lost interest. Now he was hunched over Jeremy's windowsill. Jeremy couldn't see what he was doing, but he had a bad feeling about it. "Eric," he said, "what are you doing?"

"Pulling the wings off this fly," Eric replied. "Then I'm gonna pull off his legs one by one. Then his head—"

Jeremy couldn't take it anymore. He flew at

Eric, determined to rescue the poor fly. Eric didn't even look at him. He just sent one practiced kick into Jeremy's stomach, knocking the wind out of him. As Jeremy lay on the floor, gasping for breath, Eric strolled out of his room. "Later, wuss," he said.

Jeremy looked up. The wingless, legless fly was still sitting on his windowsill, its helpless body just waiting for death.

Jeremy began to wonder if it was possible to hate anyone more than he hated Eric. The day after Eric tore apart the fly, he humiliated Jeremy at school. He called him Bug Breath in the middle of the schoolyard. Of course, the nickname had stuck. Now the entire school was calling Jeremy Bug Breath.

The next day, in the park, Eric threw a baseball at a wasps' nest. He knocked down the nest and raced into the shelter of the parks office. Three other kids were stung, though. Then Eric told the park officers that Bug Breath had knocked down the nest because he wanted it for his bug collection. The park officers had called Jeremy's mother, and Jeremy had been grounded for a week. And no sooner had Jeremy's punishment ended than the boys were stuck together again. This time at Eric's house—without a babysitter.

He's going to kill me, Jeremy thought as his mother walked him the half block to the Thompsons' house. *We'll be alone and Eric will kill me and then find a way to convince everyone that it wasn't his fault.*

But when they reached the Thompsons' house, Eric looked friendly. "Come on in," he said. "I rented a video for us. It's this cool old sci-fi thing from the seventies," he said, showing Jeremy the box. "*Attack of the Killer Bees.*"

The two mothers left, and Eric put the video in the VCR and brought out a bowl of chips. Jeremy settled himself in front of the TV. So far, so good. Maybe Eric would act human after all.

The movie was ridiculous, and Jeremy couldn't stop himself from saying so. After all, he did know a lot about bees. "They're not huge like that," he told Eric. "They're the same size as regular honeybees. It's really hard to tell them apart. And they're not dangerous when they're swarming. Their bellies are bloated with honey then, and they're not really capable of stinging. And I can't believe they set this in Mexico and have people dropping dead all over the place. I mean, in the last six years only sixty people in Mexico were reported killed by Africanized honeybees. That averages out to ten a year—not ten thousand! And this story takes place in 1972, and the Africanized bees didn't even get as far north as Mexico until 1986!"

Eric threw a pillow at him. "Will you shut up!"

"Well, it's a stupid movie," Jeremy muttered.

"One more remark and you're dead meat," Eric promised.

Jeremy held his tongue as the movie got even dumber. He couldn't believe it when one of the characters, a so-called bee expert, explained that bees avoid dark colors. Jeremy knew that bees associate blacks and browns with bears, and will often attack people wearing those colors. Eric actually thought this point was interesting. "So wearing black and brown really keeps bees away?" he asked.

"Absolutely," Jeremy replied sarcastically.

The movie finally ended with everyone in Mexico, except two brave English-speaking scientists, getting wiped out by killer bees.

Jeremy felt his stomach start to clench with tension as the credits rolled. Eric had been distracted by the movie, but it was over now. Now Eric would focus on him.

Eric turned to him and said, "Want some dinner? My mom's been insisting I cook, so I made something after I got home from school today. We just have to nuke it in the microwave."

"Sure," Jeremy said, trying not to keel over in shock. Eric offering him dinner? That dumb movie was easier to believe than Eric cooking.

Jeremy followed Eric into the kitchen. Eric opened the refrigerator door and took out two covered plastic containers. "This one's for me," he said, setting one on the counter. "And this one's for you. All you have to do is take the lid off and set it in the microwave for five minutes."

Jeremy took the lid off and then he began to scream. He kept on screaming until his throat was raw. Inside the container, on a bed of lettuce, was Gertrude, her furry black and red limbs cut into neat bite-size pieces.

Jeremy didn't talk to Eric after that. Not at school, not at the park, not even to ask him where he'd gotten his hands on Gertrude.

Jeremy simply acted as if Eric weren't there. And for a while, Eric didn't push it. He must have found someone else to pick on, Jeremy reasoned. Meanwhile, Jeremy kept studying his insects. And each month he updated the map on his wall, charting the progress of the Africanized honeybees as they moved north into the United States.

Then one day Jeremy's luck with Eric ran out. He was walking past an empty lot that was up for sale. Eric was standing in the middle of the lot, throwing stones at a dead tree. He was dressed all in black. *Like a villain,* Jeremy thought uneasily.

Jeremy looked around. There was no place to hide. Maybe Eric wouldn't notice him.

But, of course, Eric spotted him right away. "Hey, Bug Breath!" Eric called.

Jeremy walked faster, pretending that Eric didn't exist.

This time Eric wouldn't let it go. He stood directly in front of Jeremy, blocking his way. "I'm talking to you, Bug Breath," he insisted.

Jeremy tried to step around him, but Eric caught the collar of his yellow T-shirt. "I've let you live too long," he said. "Now it's time I squashed you like I squashed that hairy spider of yours."

Jeremy's eyes widened as he looked at the tree more carefully and understood why Eric had been throwing stones. There was something inside the tree.

"Uh, Eric," he said, talking fast. "You really shouldn't throw stones at that tree. It's a really bad idea because—"

"Don't tell me what to do, dork!" Eric snapped.

Jeremy tried another tactic. "Remember when I showed you that map of the Africanized honeybees?"

"Shut up, loser," Eric ordered.

Jeremy kept talking. "I was trying to tell you how far they've traveled into the U.S., where they are now."

Eric shoved him so hard he stumbled.

"But—" Jeremy's head snapped back as Eric backhanded him across the face. He felt blood trickling down the side of his mouth.

"I told you I don't care about a bunch of bees!" Eric yelled.

"Well, you ought to care," Jeremy said, blinking back tears.

"All right," Eric said, sending a fist into Jeremy's rib cage. "Where are the killer bees now?"

Jeremy's eyes were fixed on the dark cloud heading straight for Eric's back. He turned and began to run. Eric raced after him but tripped and fell to the ground.

"They're here!" Jeremy shouted as thousands of bees descended on the boy in black.

Dressed in khaki pants and his pale yellow T-shirt, Jeremy was soon far away from the empty lot and Eric's screams. He'd meant to tell Eric that it was a bad idea to attack a beehive. Especially when it belonged to Africanized honeybees and you were wearing black. But Eric wouldn't have listened, anyway.